"Are we good?"

She took a moment, then nodded. "Yeah, we're good."

"Eve..."

He wasn't sure what he meant to say to her. Maybe he just wanted to utter her name so that he had an excuse to study her upturned face, to let his gaze linger over the curve of her lips and the errant strand of auburn hair that brushed against her cheek. He resisted the urge to tuck it back. Now was not the time or place.

She cocked her head slightly. "Is there something else?"

He wondered if she'd noticed his hesitation. Wondered if she sensed the darkness that lay deep inside him. Eve could either be his salvation or his ruin and Nash wasn't about to take that gamble. "Just be careful."

His caution seemed to take her aback. Or was it something she'd read in his eyes? "Of course. I always am."

JOHN DOE
COLD CASE

———

AMANDA STEVENS

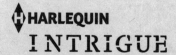

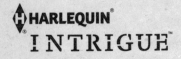

HARLEQUIN®
INTRIGUE™

ISBN-13: 978-1-335-48941-8

John Doe Cold Case

Copyright © 2022 by Marilyn Medlock Amann

This edition published by arrangement with Harlequin Books S.A.

For questions and comments about the quality of this book, please contact us at CustomerService@Harlequin.com.

Harlequin Enterprises ULC
22 Adelaide St. West, 41st Floor
Toronto, Ontario M5H 4E3, Canada
www.Harlequin.com

Printed in U.S.A.

Amanda Stevens is an award-winning author of over fifty novels, including the modern gothic series The Graveyard Queen. Her books have been described as eerie and atmospheric, and "a new take on the classic ghost story." Born and raised in the rural South, she now resides in Houston, Texas, where she enjoys binge-watching, bike riding and the occasional margarita.

Books by Amanda Stevens

Harlequin Intrigue

A Procedural Crime Story

Little Girl Gone
John Doe Cold Case

An Echo Lake Novel

Without a Trace
A Desperate Search
Someone Is Watching

Twilight's Children

Criminal Behavior
Incriminating Evidence
Killer Investigation
Pine Lake
Whispering Springs
Bishop's Rock (ebook novella)

MIRA

The Graveyard Queen

The Restorer
The Kingdom
The Prophet
The Visitor
The Sinner
The Awakening

Visit the Author Profile page at Harlequin.com.

CAST OF CHARACTERS

Eve Jareau—When the skeletal remains of a John Doe are discovered deep inside a cave on the outskirts of Black Creek, Florida, Detective Jareau is excited by the prospect of solving another old murder...until the clues lead her too close to home.

Nash Bowden—A disastrous marriage and bitter divorce have left him wary and distrustful. So when he suspects Detective Jareau is withholding information in a criminal investigation, he vows to uncover her secrets...no matter what it costs him.

John Doe—The holed coin found in the grave of a murder victim threatens to turn Eve's world upside down.

Jackie Jareau—Twenty-eight years ago, her handsome, charming husband left her for another woman. Did his betrayal drive her to do the unthinkable?

Wayne Brody—Eve's ex-stepfather seems to have an unhealthy obsession with her mother. How far is he willing to go to remain in her life?

Nadine Crosby—The other woman and a co-conspirator in an unspeakable crime.

Denton Crosby—A man who will do anything to keep his dastardly deed from coming to light.

Chapter One

Deep inside a cave near Black Creek, Florida, the skeletal remains of a John Doe had remained hidden for nearly three decades. The forensic anthropologist called in by the local police chief estimated the deceased's age at time of death to be late twenties. He'd been tall, thin and right-handed. Good teeth, strong bones. And he'd been brutally murdered. Bashed in the back of the head and stabbed multiple times in the chest.

Overkill, Detective Eve Jareau thought with an inward grimace as she stood gazing down at the skeleton carefully arranged in the supine position on a metal table. The crawling flesh at the back of her neck surprised her. She wasn't a stranger to death. In the six years she'd been with the Black Creek Police Department, she'd witnessed the gamut from shootings to car wrecks to natural causes. Why these unidentified skeletal remains should have such a visceral effect was inexplicable.

Maybe it was her surroundings, she decided. The building that housed the forensic anthropology lab was old and creaky with too many lurking shadows. Despite the overhead lights, a perpetual gloom seemed to linger over the tables of weathered bones and shelves of forensic artifacts. The downpour pelting against the long windows did nothing to lighten her mood. Eve suppressed another shiver as she glanced at her boss, police chief Nash Bowden, who stood on the opposite side of the table. Whether aware of her scrutiny or not, he didn't glance up.

His disconnect was par for the course these days. He'd avoided eye contact and all but cursory conversation for the entire forty-five-minute drive from Black Creek to Tallahassee. Eve told herself she shouldn't take it personally. He'd always kept to himself. However, ever since his ex-wife had been arrested for the kidnapping of a four-year-old child, he'd retreated deeper behind his impenetrable walls. Thankfully, the little girl had been rescued and returned to her mother unharmed, but the whole town still reeled from the revelation. Eve could only imagine the blow it must have been to Chief Bowden—Nash.

Once upon a time, there'd been a spark between Eve and Nash. A fleeting moment of possibility that had fizzled in the face of his difficult divorce and the complicated reality of a workplace relationship. Still, something lingered in spite of the obstacles. Eve had to squelch the desire to reassure him that the kidnapping wasn't his fault. No one could have seen that coming. Instead, she'd wisely held her silence even when he'd called her into his office to offer her lead on the John Doe case.

The assignment was hardly a testament to her skills.

No one else wanted the case. The seasoned investigators didn't have the patience or the inclination to put in the hours of tedious research and legwork that a cold case generally required, and the younger, more ambitious detectives were eager to nab the hot cases. Eve marched to a different drummer. Neither jaded nor single-minded, she enjoyed the challenge of a decades-old puzzle. She preferred working quietly and alone.

Forcing her attention back to the matter at hand, she watched in fascination as Dr. Allison Forester rotated the disarticulated skull to highlight the spiderweb pattern at the base.

"I suppose there's no way of knowing whether the blunt force trauma occurred before or after the stabbing," Nash said.

"Unfortunately, no." Dr. Forester ran a gloved finger over the deep indentation. "But a blow this traumatic would have incapacitated, if not killed him outright. Likewise, some of the stab wounds were deep and forceful enough to almost sever his ribs."

Nash nodded his understanding. "You're saying the victim suffered multiple mortal wounds. If he was already dead or dying from the head trauma, why stab him so viciously?"

"Rage," Eve muttered.

His gaze met hers briefly before he glanced away.

"Maybe he was trying to get away," Dr. Forester suggested. "The blow from behind was meant to finish him off."

A terrible vision swirled in Eve's head. The victim bleeding and near death, but still trying to crawl away from his attacker. He would never have seen the death blow coming.

Dr. Forester repositioned the skull and then moved to the side of the table to stand next to Nash. She was a striking woman with ash-blond hair and gray-green eyes. Every now and then, Eve caught her watching Nash through her thick lashes. Now she moved in close enough so that her arm brushed against his. He didn't retreat, Eve noted. In fact, if anything, he seemed to lean into her.

The subtle intimacy distracted her for a moment until she sternly reminded herself to stay focused. *This is none of your business.* But she couldn't help noting how Nash's dark eyes and hair complemented the woman's cool blondness.

A clap of thunder rattled the windows and Eve ran a hand up and down her arm where goose bumps rose among the freckles. *Who are you?* she wondered as she dropped her gaze to the skeleton. *And what were you doing down in that cave?*

The rolling thunder seemed ominous, like the harbinger of something dark and chaotic. When the lights flickered, Eve could have sworn an icy finger touched the back of her hand. She actually checked to make sure the skeleton hadn't moved. Then she chided herself for letting a storm and some old bones unsettle her.

"You okay?"

She glanced up at Nash's query. "What?"

His gaze seemed unusually intense. "You seem jumpy."

Her heart thudded despite her resolve as she glanced

around the lab. "This place is a little too atmospheric for my taste."

"You get used to it." Dr. Forester's lowered voice sent another ripple across Eve's nerve endings. "After a while, you don't even notice the strange noises and electrical fluctuations."

"What kind of strange noises?"

The woman merely smiled. "At least we don't have to worry about working in the dark. We have a backup generator."

"That's good to know," Eve murmured.

"If it still works, that is. We may need a volunteer to go down in the basement and check the controls."

"This building has a basement? Doesn't it flood?" Eve asked.

"She's putting you on," Nash said.

"Oh."

Dr. Forester's eyes gleamed. "Only about the basement. I'm dead serious about the odd anomalies. If you spend enough time in this building, you're bound to experience something you can't explain."

Like the brush of a skeletal hand?

Eve couldn't tell if the woman was being serious or not. She decided to shrug off the nebulous warning. "Maybe we should finish up before the lights really do go out."

"Yes, that's probably a good idea." Dr. Forester exchanged an amused glance with Nash before she bent back to her work. She pointed out two places in the right radius and carpus before moving down the torso to the right tibia and the lower portion of the left fibula. "At some point in his life, our John Doe sustained multiple fractures to his right arm and leg and his left ankle, possibly from an automobile accident. He received medical treatment. The breaks fused cleanly."

"If he was treated locally, hospital records could help with the identification," Nash said. "Once we go public with the discovery, a relative or acquaintance may come forward."

"John Doe was down in that cave for decades," Eve said. "It's possible his family moved away from the area years ago."

"All speculation at this point." Nash turned back to Dr. Forester. "Anything else? What about clothing or jewelry recovered from the excavation site?"

"Bits and pieces of fabric and leather. No wallet. Nothing with an inscription. We did find something interesting, however." She pulled a small evidence bag from a drawer in the table. Dumping the contents into her palm, she picked up a small silver coin and held it between her thumb and forefinger.

Nash lifted a brow. "A dime?"

Dr. Forester swiveled the coin so that the tarnished silver caught a bit of light. "A Mercury dime with a small perforation at the top. The deceased probably wore it on a string around his neck or ankle for good luck. It's an old Southern superstition that dates back before the Civil War."

"I've never heard of that particular superstition," Nash said.

Dr. Forester gave him a knowing look. "I'm not surprised. You've never struck me as the mystical sort. Detective Jareau, on the other hand…"

Eve remained silent, her heart thudding in trepidation. *No, it can't be true. It's simply not possible.*

"You know anything about Mercury dimes?" Nash's voice tunneled through the cloud of dread that had descended.

"Only that they're collectible, depending on the condition," she mumbled with a shrug, but already an old memory had seeped out of her subconscious. She was in her childhood bedroom staring up at the glow-in-the-dark stars on her ceiling when her father called softly from the doorway, "Boo? You awake?"

She'd turned toward his voice. "Yes, Daddy."

"Shush. Let's not wake your mama." He came in and sat down on the edge of her bed, keeping his tone hushed. "I'm going away for a while, Boo. I didn't want to leave without saying goodbye."

Eve felt a stab of panic as she pushed herself up against the pillows. "Where are you going?"

"Back to Louisiana, where I grew up. One of my cousins has offered me a job down in New Orleans. I'll likely be gone for a good long while."

"Can't Mama and me come with you?"

"Not this time. You need to stay here and look after each other. Can you do that, Boo?"

"Yes, Daddy."

"That's my good girl." He smiled down at her as he brushed an unruly lock of dark hair from his forehead. "I've got something for you. Kind of like a going-away present." He reached in his pocket and brought out a dime threaded on a piece of twine.

The coin shone in the moonlight as he dangled the string.

Eve let out an awed breath. "Your good-luck charm!"

"No, *your* good-luck charm. I still have mine. See?" He pulled the silver coin from his collar. "My daddy found it for me when I was your age and now I've found one for you. Mercury dimes in general are hard to come by, but one with a hole is even more special. Do you know why?"

She shook her head.

"Most people don't know about the power of certain coins. But someone a hundred years ago figured out this particular dime held a lot of good juju. They punched a hole in the top so they could wear it close to their heart for luck and protection." He put the coin in Eve's hand and closed her fingers around it. "It's our secret, okay? No need to tell Mama. She'll think it's just a silly superstition."

"I won't tell."

"Each night before you go to bed, stand at the window with that lucky dime. Look up at the moon and think about me. I'll be gazing up at the same moon and thinking about you. That way, we'll always be together no matter where we are."

He tucked her in and left the room, but Eve couldn't sleep. Her daddy was going away and she had a terrible feeling he was never coming back.

She threw off the covers and stole over to the window to stare out. A car was parked at the curb. She watched in fascination as her father ran down the front steps carrying a small suitcase in one hand and a paper bag in the other. He hurried down the sidewalk to the car, then opened the trunk and stored everything inside. He went around and got in on the passenger side. When the interior light came on, Eve saw a woman with short platinum hair behind the wheel and the silhouette of a man in the back seat.

A split second before the door closed and the light went out, the man turned to stare back at the house, searching through the shadows until his gaze met hers. He put a finger to his lips and then drew that same finger across his throat. Eve hadn't known then what the gesture meant, but the look on his face had terrified her. She'd wanted nothing so much as to climb out the window and run after her daddy, but instead she shrank back in the shadows and waited until the taillights of the strange car had disappeared down the street before crawling back into bed and pulling the covers over her head.

"Detective Jareau? Your thoughts?"

Nash's voice once again cut into her reverie, dragging her back into the spooky lab.

She lifted her gaze. "About the dime, you mean?"

"About the injuries, the dime, everything we've learned today." His eyes narrowed as if he'd read her mind.

Eve shrugged off the memory and stared back at him. "You're right about the injuries. That many old breaks could be key to identifying the victim. I'll enter all the information in the database as soon as we get back to the station."

Nash's enigmatic focus lingered before he said to Dr. Forester, "You'll let us know if you find anything else?"

"Of course." Her hand fluttered to his sleeve. "A word before you go?"

He hesitated almost infinitesimally, then tossed his key fob to Eve. "I'll meet you outside."

At any other time, she might have bristled at the dismissal, but now she welcomed the opportunity to escape. She gave a curt nod and turned toward the exit without a backward glance at the bones.

Out in the hallway, she made sure she was alone before leaning against the wall and closing her eyes as she fingered the Mercury dime beneath her T-shirt. It had to be a coincidence. Her father had sent money to her mother and postcards to Eve after he'd left town. If he'd come back to Black Creek for whatever reason, surely he would have let them know. Surely he would have wanted to see his only child. The same little girl who had once thought the sun rose and set on her capricious father.

It's not him.

Eve's mother had always believed her husband had run off with another woman. Eve knew this because she'd once overheard Jackie Jareau confide in a friend that her husband had had a wandering eye ever since she'd known him. No doubt he was living a new life somewhere with a second family, her mother had lamented. He probably never gave a passing thought to the wife and child he'd left behind in Black Creek.

Despite that overheard conversation, Eve had never wanted to believe the reality of her father's abandonment. She'd desperately clung to the hope that he was out there somewhere, thinking about her every time he looked up at the moon.

Nearly three decades later, she still wanted to believe. Gabriel Jareau hadn't been savagely murdered and buried beneath a pile of rubble in some godforsaken cave. The Mercury dime was just a coincidence.

The lights in the hallway sputtered as if to disparage her fantasy. Unnerved, Eve glanced up at the flickering bulbs as she pressed herself against the wall. She didn't hear or see anything out of the ordinary, but an unnatural chill from the rain seemed to ooze in through the windows and doors. She had to fight the urge to flee back into the lab.

Hurrying down the hallway instead, she pushed open the glass double doors and then paused once more beneath the covered entrance, wishing she'd brought an umbrella. The rain was really coming down now as thunder rumbled overhead. It wasn't yet six in the evening—normally still daylight in the summertime—but the sky had already deepened.

The parking lot was nearly empty. No one was about on the walkways, either. Eve glanced back through the glass doors, hoping to see Nash striding toward the entrance. Nothing but shadows lurked in the corridor.

Why was she so nervous all of a sudden? What was she really afraid of? She was armed, trained and prepared to take care of herself when and if the situation warranted. No reason for her jitters. But she was also Gabriel Jareau's daughter, superstitious and eccentric to a fault. Like her father, Eve believed in signs and portents and she knew without knowing how she knew that something was about to go terribly wrong in her world.

Leaving the shelter of the overhang, she dashed across the drenched parking lot. As she sprinted around to the passenger side of Nash's SUV, she noticed that the interior light was on in a car a few spaces over. Something about the man's profile reminded her of the silhouette in the back seat the night her father had left home. Impossible, of course. Even if she'd seen the stranger clearly that night, she'd only been five years old and he would have changed beyond recognition in the nearly three decades that had passed. Still…there was something about *this* man…

As if drawn by Eve's scrutiny, he glanced up, and she could have sworn he put a finger to his lips a split second before the interior light went out.

It's nothing, she told herself. Just a man waiting for someone who worked in the building.

Then why had he turned off the light when he saw her? Why had he gestured her to silence? Or had he? Maybe the storm and her old memories were playing tricks.

A hand fell on her shoulder and she jumped.

"What are you doing standing out here in the rain?" Nash asked. "Didn't I give you the key?"

"You did. I was just…" She shook her head. "Nothing. It doesn't matter."

He cast an uneasy glance at the sky. "I don't think this storm is going to let up anytime soon. We should probably hit the road before it gets worse."

"Chief…"

Raindrops glistened on his lashes as he gazed down at her. "What is it?"

She wanted to tell him about her childhood memory and about the dime she wore around her neck. She wanted to mention the man in the car and explain the uncanny certainty that something dark was headed her way. But she wasn't yet ready to accept the possibility of John Doe's identity. She needed to talk to her mother first.

"You're right," she said on a breath. "We should get going before things get worse."

NASH CHECKED THE rearview as he exited the freeway onto the two-lane blacktop that would take them straight into Black Creek. The rain had momentarily slackened, but lightning flickered from a new bank of clouds that gathered on the horizon.

Traffic was light on the highway. If he wasn't careful, he could too easily fall into one of his dark moods, lulled by the rhythmic swish of the wiper blades. He lifted a hand and rubbed the back of his neck. He hadn't been sleeping well lately. Ever since his ex-wife had been apprehended for the kidnapping of little Kylie Buchanan, the old nightmares had returned—the same bad dreams that had followed him home from Afghanistan nearly twelve years ago and still squatted in the blackest corners of his subconscious.

Kylie was now safely home with her mother, and Grace had been transferred from county lockup to a mental health facility in Tallahassee for psychiatric evaluation. Nash hadn't been to see her yet, nor did he want to. The separation and divorce had dragged on for far too long—Grace had seen to that—and left him bitter. He bit back a lingering resentment for all those wasted years and reminded himself that his former wife was a troubled woman.

No matter how hard he tried, though, he couldn't rustle up much sympathy. What she'd put that little girl and her family through was unforgivable. Still, she'd saved Nash's life once and he didn't take that lightly.

Beside him, Eve stirred restlessly. She'd been quiet ever since they left the lab, but then he wasn't making conversation easy for her. He felt a pang of regret that he quickly crushed. Keeping Eve Jareau at arm's length had always been for the best. He had too much baggage going back even before Grace. Now more than ever he needed to keep that space between them, for her sake as well as his own.

"It wasn't your fault, you know."

The softness of Eve's tone drilled deep into his defenses. Her head was turned toward the window. He wondered for a moment if he might have imagined her comment. "I'm sorry. Did you say something?"

"What she did is no reflection on you."

He drew a sharp breath, caught off guard yet again by the power of her voice. "I doubt many people would agree with you about that."

"You're wrong. No one blames you. No one that matters."

She turned just as he shot her a glance. Their gazes met, held and then each looked away quickly, but not before her blue eyes revealed a naked longing that clawed right through Nash's resolve.

His hands tightened on the wheel. "I should have known."

"How could you?" Eve demanded. "You're not clairvoyant."

"If I'd paid more attention to the clues, I would have seen it coming. I would have figured out what she was up to."

Eve seemed to consider and discard the possibility. "I don't think you're giving Grace enough credit. It was very clever of her to emulate an old kidnapping in order to make it look as though the two crimes were connected. She forced us to consider the possibility that the same kidnapper who took little Maya Lamb twenty-eight years ago came back to take Kylie Buchanan. Not to mention all the evidence she planted that threw everyone off her trail, including the FBI. She fooled a lot of people. She had us chasing shadows for days. What happened wasn't your fault."

He drew a hand across his eyes. "I appreciate what you're trying to do, but I'd rather not talk about Grace, if you don't mind." *Not with you. Not with anyone.*

"Of course. I understand…"

He lifted a brow. "But?"

"You need to talk to someone. Keeping everything bottled up inside isn't healthy."

"Speaking from experience?"

"Speaking as a friend."

Why did her voice get to him so? It was soft, yes, but there was grit around the edges. He admired her toughness and determination. He admired a great many things about Eve Jareau, not the least of which were more shallow observations. The soft curves beneath the jeans and T-shirt. The scent of rosemary and mint that seemed to envelop him. The large SUV afforded plenty of space between them. No way he could smell her soap and shampoo from across the console, but somehow the clean scent of her hair and skin lingered in his memory.

He scowled at the road. "You didn't say much back at the lab. I'm surprised you didn't have more questions for Dr. Forester."

"Oh, I have plenty of questions."

He gave her a sidelong glance. Something about the shift in her tone triggered a faint concern. "Anything I should know about?"

She hesitated. "For starters, what was the victim doing down in that cave? He must have been lured there somehow. The cavern where the remains were found is hard to get to. The body wasn't just dumped there."

Nash nodded. "I've been through those tunnels. It's tough going under any circumstances, but it would be next to impossible to drag the body of a grown man through all those belly-crawls. Someone lured him back into that cavern and ambushed him. It's up to you to find out who and why."

She gave a sharp nod. "And I will."

Nash wondered if she felt as confident as she

sounded. Maybe it was his imagination, but she seemed moody and pensive. On edge. What was going on with her anyway?

"Once we have Dr. Forester's full report, we'll release the findings to the press," he said. "Hopefully, someone will come forward. Even after all these years, I wouldn't discount the possibility that someone saw something."

She brushed a twig of hair behind her ears as she nodded. "That would certainly make my job easier. As for why I didn't have more questions for Dr. Forester, she was very thorough in her explanation."

"She knows her stuff," Nash agreed.

"You've worked with her before?"

The question was innocent enough, but Nash sensed something deeper than curiosity in the query. "A few times when I was with the Tallahassee PD." He wouldn't get into the coffee dates he'd shared with Allison Forester during his separation or the casual hookups since his divorce. Neither of them wanted a serious relationship, and Allie's go-with-the-flow attitude was just what he'd needed. His disastrous marriage had left him gunshy, which was only one of many reasons he needed to keep Eve Jareau at arm's length and then some.

"I see," she murmured.

He gave her another side glance before returning his attention to the road. The rain was starting to come down again and he needed to stay focused. The pavement could get deceptively slippery in places. "How far are you in the missing-persons files?"

"It's a slog," she said. "The physical files are in bad shape. I may need to recruit some help."

"Resources are tight. We can only allocate so much to a case this old."

She turned with a frown. "Are you saying I'm on my own?"

"I'll give you as much help as I can, but we have to be realistic."

Not the answer she wanted, obviously, but he had a tight budget and a frugal mayor to appease.

"I'd like to go down in the cave," she said. "That won't cost anything but my time."

Her response surprised him. "What do you hope to find? We went all through those tunnels after Kylie Buchanan disappeared, and Forensics combed through the cavern after the remains were excavated. I doubt you'll find anything useful."

"I'd still like to see that cavern for myself."

He nodded. "Fair enough. I'll contact the property owner as soon as we get back to the station and make the arrangements. He's planning on sealing the entrances permanently since the body was recovered, but I'm sure he can adjust the schedule to accommodate our investigation. I'll let you know what he says, but we'll need to wait for the weather to clear regardless."

"We?"

He could feel her curious gaze on him. "I'll run point. I'm not trying to micromanage your case," he hurriedly added before she could protest. "Like I said, I've recently been through all those tunnels. It's easy to get turned around if you're unfamiliar with the layout. As soon as we get the go-ahead, we'll need to arrange for proper equipment and backup. After everything that's happened, I don't want to allow even the smallest margin for error. Last thing we need is for something to go wrong down in that cave."

She nodded. "I never thanked you for giving me this case. I suspect it was more or less by default, but I appreciate the opportunity just the same."

"There was no default. I made you lead because you're a smart, diligent investigator. You're also tireless and you work well alone. But a case this old will require a lot of patience," he warned. "Besides the limited resources, you'll be following a trail that went cold years ago. Any leads you manage to turn up will need to be tracked down between your other cases. John Doe just isn't a priority."

"He is to me."

Nash shot her another glance, but the telltale bump and thud of a flat tire quelled his response. The vehicle careened toward the right and he swore under his breath as he gripped the wheel. "Great. Just what we need on a night like this."

"There was a lot of construction back at the lab. We probably ran over a nail." He saw her glance back at the road and he could have sworn she suppressed a shiver. "Do we have a spare?"

"Yeah. Let's hope it has air." He gently pumped the brakes and guided the vehicle off the road onto the narrow shoulder. He turned on his emergency flashers as he glanced in the rearview mirror. "Luckily there's not much traffic, but I can see the glow of headlights on the horizon. Put out the reflectors while I grab the spare."

They both climbed out and met at the rear of the vehicle. While Eve placed the triangular reflectors several yards from the SUV in both directions, Nash lifted the spare from the rack and got to work. Positioning his flashlight on the soggy shoulder, he used a tire iron to loosen the lug nuts.

Once the reflectors were set, Eve shouted over the rain, "Anything else I can do?"

"Keep an eye out for that oncoming vehicle." He glanced her way as he finished loosening the lug nuts. She'd walked some distance from the SUV and stood on the shoulder waving her flashlight beam back and forth on the ground to alert the approaching vehicle. The car was still some distance away, but she wasn't taking any chances. Nash liked that about her. Cautious and meticulous were good qualities in a detective, though he knew firsthand she had a reckless streak she kept well hidden. He'd glimpsed it once when she kissed him unexpectedly. They'd blamed the incident on adrenaline and had never spoken of it again. But he'd thought about it over the years. Sometimes he thought about that kiss a lot.

Once he had the spare on, he hand-tightened the lug nuts, lowered the jack and used the tire tool to secure the bolts. By this time, the glare from the headlights reflecting off raindrops was blinding. Was it his imagination or had the car picked up speed?

He shouted a warning to Eve. She glanced back at him a split second before the car swerved toward the shoulder. She went down so quickly Nash was momentarily stunned. Then he leaped to his feet and rushed toward the spot where he'd last seen her.

The vehicle didn't stop or even slow. Instead, the driver gunned the engine and the car skidded violently toward Nash so that he had to dive out of the way. The car smashed into the nearest reflectors and sideswiped the SUV as the rear end fishtailed on the wet pavement. The sound of metal grinding against metal sent a chill up Nash's spine. He witnessed the collision in his periphery as he stumbled to his feet and sprinted through the torrent.

"Detective Jareau! Eve!"

He didn't see her at first. Had she been thrown down the embankment?

He swept his flashlight all along the shoulder and then down the rugged incline. She lay facedown at the bottom.

He took a quick survey over his shoulder. The car sped down the highway, the taillights already a blur in the rain.

Half running, half sliding, Nash descended the embankment and knelt beside Eve. She wasn't moving. "Can you hear me?" He heard a low groan over the downpour and his pounding heart. "Eve!"

She rolled onto her back and stared up at him. Raindrops splashed against her face. He tried to shelter her as best he could with his body. "Were you hit?"

"No, I slipped. I'm okay, I think. Just stunned."

"Don't try to move until we know for sure."

But she was already struggling to sit up. "The car

didn't touch me. My feet slid out from under me when I jumped back. Next thing I knew I was rolling down the embankment." She put a hand to a scrape on her cheek. "Ouch."

"Are you sure the car didn't hit you?"

"Yes, but not for lack of trying. Did you see the way he swerved toward the shoulder? I didn't imagine that, did I?"

"No, I had to jump out the way, too. He hit my vehicle and kept going. It's possible the flashlight and reflectors disoriented him." Nash had seen it before. Sometimes in panic, people drove straight toward the object they were trying to avoid. He grasped her elbow and helped her to her feet.

"I couldn't get the plate number. Everything happened too fast, and the rain and headlights blinded me." She wiped her hands on the seat of her jeans. "What about you?"

"Just the first two letters. The vehicle looked to be a dark late-model sedan, which doesn't help much. Like you said, it happened too quickly and visibility was severely limited by the rain and glare of headlights." He checked her out in the flashlight beam. "Are you sure you're okay? That's a nasty scrape on your cheek."

She put her hand up to the tender spot and flinched. "I've had worse. Do you think your vehicle is drivable?"

"We'll soon find out. In any case, we should probably get everything off the road. I'll grab the tire and jack while you pick up the reflectors."

"Nash?"

He noticed she didn't call him chief. "Yes?"

She fingered a tiny silver chain at her throat. "I guess it's a good thing I wore my good-luck charm today."

Chapter Two

Nash was still in his office when Eve left the station later that evening. She glimpsed him at his desk through the glass partition that separated his office from the squad room. His head was bowed to his work and he seemed utterly absorbed in whatever he was doing. He didn't glance up when she paused outside his door. She wanted to ask if he'd had a chance to contact Mr. McNally about a cave excursion, but instead, she moved on without knocking. Best not to disturb him. Besides, she had other things on her mind at the moment.

Earlier, when they'd finally arrived back in town, she'd managed to convince him she really was okay. No cuts, no breaks. No need to go to the ER. Just the scrape on her cheek, which she'd cleaned and disinfected in the bathroom. Then, after changing out of her wet clothes into the spare set she kept in her locker, she'd settled in at her desk to update the database with Dr. Forester's findings and then to pore through the boxes of physical missing-persons files she'd brought up from the archives.

The task had proved frustrating in more ways than

one. The folders were fragile and smelled of mildew from a flood ten years ago. The ink was so badly smeared on some of the reports as to render them illegible. Pages were stuck together or missing altogether. Labels had come unglued and fallen to the bottom of the file boxes. Before Eve knew it, two hours had rolled by and she'd barely made a dent in her search. She considered working another hour or two, but her muscles were already aching, so she decided to call it a night and start fresh in the morning.

Leaving the station, she cut across the parking lot to her car, glancing around for any vehicles that didn't belong and for any tinted windows that might hide watchful eyes. She hated feeling so paranoid. Nash was probably right about the panicked driver on the highway. The flashing lights and reflectors had disoriented him. And the guy in the parking lot at the lab was just a guy in a parking lot. Both cars had been dark-colored sedans, but so what? Plenty of vehicles on the road matching that description. She wouldn't have given either incident a passing consideration if not for the holed coin that had been found with the remains and the disturbing memory that had come creeping out of her subconscious.

The discovery of the skeleton wasn't yet public knowledge, but word had a way of traveling fast through a small town. What if the killer knew his victim had been dug up? Was he even now watching Eve's every move?

Chiding herself for her overactive imagination, she scrubbed a hand across her eyes. She was tired, verg-

ing on punch-drunk. The whole department had been
running on nothing but adrenaline since little Kylie Buchanan's abduction. Now that the child had been found
safe and sound, it was time to take a breath.

Eve drove through the wet streets with music stream-
ing softly from the sound system. Darkness seemed
to close in on her. Every shadow, every drooping tree
branch caught her attention as the hair rose on the back
of her neck. Overreaction or not, she couldn't shake
the dark foreboding that had dogged her since leaving the lab.

It wasn't just the niggling worry of bad things to
come, though. She felt restive, empty and a bit gloomy.
Much of her off-duty time was spent alone, but she
rarely felt lonely. She always had friends and family
nearby when she needed them. Tonight, however, she
experienced a strange hollowness in her chest that she
couldn't explain and a creeping uneasiness that kept
her glancing in the rearview mirror.

John Doe's possible identity wore heavily on her.
She didn't like keeping secrets from Nash, but honestly,
what did she really know at this point? If she confided
her suspicion, he might feel obligated to remove her
from the case, and that was the last thing she wanted.
No one else would devote the time and energy necessary to solve an old homicide. And solve it she would,
no matter what she had to do to get at the truth.

After pulling into her garage, she sat until her favorite song ended before lowering the overhead door. Then
she exited through the side entrance into the backyard.
It was a warm, humid evening. The rain had stopped,

and a few stars twinkled. The air hung heavy with the scent of jasmine and honeysuckle, and the dull ache in her chest deepened. She paused once more, lifting her face to the shrouded moon as she fingered the dime beneath her shirt.

Daddy, are you there?

The breeze picked up, drifting through the leaves overhead and resurrecting an unnerving sense of being watched. Eve scoured the backyard, probing the bushes and shadowy corners, but no one lurked, living or dead. No one that she could see anyway.

She shivered, stroking a hand down her arm where goose bumps had once again popped. The sensation wasn't unfamiliar. For most of her life, she'd sensed a mysterious presence. On occasion, she would sometimes wake up in the middle of the night with a cold, dreaded certainty that someone watched her from the dark. When she was little, she would huddle under the covers till daybreak, but as she grew older, she'd sometimes get up and pad to the window to boldly search the shadows. Once, she'd seen someone staring back at her. She'd never told her mother about the interloper and to this day, she couldn't explain why. For one thing, she hadn't wanted to cause undue fear or worry, but something else, an indefinable need for secrecy, had kept her silent.

Don't tell your mama. She wouldn't understand.

Shrugging off the melancholy and her father's phantom caution, Eve hurried up the steps and unlocked the back door, casting a final glance over her shoulder before scurrying inside. Piling her belongings on the kitchen island, she considered having a drink to settle her nerves, but she hadn't eaten since lunch. Alcohol on an empty stomach was never a good idea. Besides, she still had business to attend to that evening. After fixing a hasty sandwich, she showered, dressed and headed out again, this time on foot.

Her mother lived two blocks over in the same house where Eve had grown up. The windows in the seventies ranch-style house were dark. Her mother must still be at work, she decided. Jackie Jareau's boss was a clinical psychologist who conducted group therapy sessions two evenings a week. Jackie stayed after-hours on those days so that Dr. Gail Mercer wouldn't be alone in the office with her patients.

Eve glanced at her phone. Just after nine. Surely her mother would be home soon. She sent a text just in case.

Hey, where are you?

Her mother responded immediately. Just leaving the office. What's up?

I'm at your place. I was hoping we could talk tonight if you're not too tired.

Never too tired for you. Everything okay?

Yes, I just want to see you.

Use the spare key. I'll be home in a few.

Eve went around to the back and collected the key from the hiding spot above the door. She let herself in and walked through the darkened house and down the narrow hallway to her old bedroom. Turning on a lamp, she glanced around. The bare bones of the room had changed little since she'd left home. The posters were gone, along with the garish lime-green wall color she'd once favored. Her mother had painted everything over in crisp white and replaced the bed linens with something more neutral and grown-up. But the furniture was the same and Jackie had sentimentally left all the stars on the ceiling. If Eve lay on the bed, she could still watch them twinkle as moonlight reflected off the foil.

Opening a dresser drawer, she rifled through the contents until she found the photograph of her father that had once rested on her nightstand. She carried the frame over to the bed and sat on the edge as she studied the photograph.

Twenty-eight years had passed since she'd last seen him. Almost a lifetime for Eve. A daddy's girl to her very core, she'd barely been five when he left. She'd adored him so, clinging to his hand when they went out, wrapping her arms around his legs when he returned home from one of his trips. Even after all these years, Eve remembered vividly Gabriel Jareau's snapping eyes and unruly hair. His mischievous smile and teasing manner. If she concentrated hard enough, she could still hear traces of his Cajun roots in his rich baritone.

She drew a thumb across the glass that protected his image. Her father had been a charming, handsome man. Tall, thin, right-handed. Good bones, good teeth.

Eve let out a slow breath as she fell back against the mattress and stared up at the peeling stars. She must have dozed off because she heard her father say clearly, "Boo? You awake?"

Bolting upright, she glanced around. The voice had been a dream, but the creaking floorboards somewhere in the house were real.

NASH DROVE STRAIGHT home after he left the station. He'd thought about stopping somewhere for takeout— Mexican or Cuban always hit the spot—but he experienced a strange sense of urgency that propelled him through the darkened streets, intensifying into a prickle at the back of his neck as he turned into the narrow driveway at his house. He cut the lights and sat for a moment scouring the property.

He didn't know why he felt so on edge. Eve's close call out on the highway had scared the hell out of him, but she was okay. Just banged up a little. This was something different. A gnawing foreboding that the other shoe was about to drop.

Could be nothing more than his imagination, he decided. An amplified dread brought on by the lingering strain of Grace's arrest and the icy realization of just how devious and cruel his ex-wife could truly be.

She'd planned the kidnapping meticulously, taking the little girl through the same bedroom window from which another child had vanished twenty-eight years ago. Then she'd stashed four-year-old Kylie in a remote cabin while finalizing her plans to leave the country. Despite everything Grace had done to Nash over the years, the untold grief she'd brought into his life, he would never have thought her capable of something so dark.

Though, to be honest, he'd seen signs of her malice long before the divorce. She'd tried any number of ploys during their separation to lure him back into her web. He'd succumbed too many times to her deceitful machinations out of guilt, weakness and the fear that he'd somehow been responsible for pushing her to the brink. No more. Now was not the time to backslide into his own dark place. He'd come too far and he had too many responsibilities. He had a town to protect and an old homicide to solve.

He'd assigned the case to Eve because he trusted her to do everything in her power to solve it. But already Nash had insinuated himself into the investigation, arranging the consultation earlier with Allison Forester and then suggesting that he and Eve drive over to Tallahassee together. She hadn't objected, but he wondered if she could see through his motives. Despite his resolve to keep his distance, he was doing everything in his power to draw her back into his orbit.

Not smart. She was too good a woman to get involved with a man whose night terrors still woke him up in a cold sweat, whose baggage was sometimes like a dead weight resting on his shoulders. A man who every now and then seemed one drink away from ending up facedown in a gutter.

He shook off his gloom and let himself into the house. Flipping on the light, he tossed his keys in the wooden bowl he kept on a small table near the door.

Then glancing out the window, he hung up his holster and took care of his weapon. Despite the fact that he lived alone, habit dictated that he lock his gun in the safe and slide the key back into its hiding place.

There'd been a time not so long ago when he couldn't trust a bolted door to keep Grace from entering his home in the middle of the night and stealing through the darkened rooms. He'd once awakened to find her at the foot of his bed with a 9 mm aimed at his heart. After that, he'd made sure to secure both the weapons he owned before he went to sleep at night, and he'd had the locks changed on every door in the house. Even so, Grace had her ways. Sometimes when he came home from work, he could still sense her presence.

She couldn't get to him now. She couldn't hurt herself or anyone he loved, but Nash knew he wouldn't rest until he searched the house. Old habits really did die hard.

He started in the living area and made his way down the hallway, peering into the bedrooms and bathrooms until he reached the last door. The moment he entered the small room he'd converted into a home office, he knew something was wrong.

A warm breeze drifted through the open slider. He hadn't left it unlocked. He would never be that careless. It was possible the cleaning service he used might have neglected to close the door, but he'd never had any problem with them before.

He took in the room at a glance and then eased to his desk, removing the backup firearm he kept locked in the top drawer. Then he slipped through the door onto the concrete patio, his gaze scouring the bushes and all along the wooden fence.

Keeping to the shadows, he tuned his senses to the night. A dog barked down the street. A car horn sounded in the distance. He listened for the longest moment before he walked the yard, looking for evidence of an intruder. Then he backtracked to the office and examined the lock. No sign of a break-in. No footprints beneath the windows. Nothing. And yet he knew someone had been inside his house.

He went back into the office and turned on the overhead light. He'd left a few files stacked neatly on his desk. One of the folders contained his notes and copies of the photographs taken deep inside the cave where the bones had been discovered. Nash had kept hard copies for himself when he handed the electronic file over to Eve, though he wasn't sure why. He trusted her skill and instincts, but something about this particular John Doe bothered him.

The tingle at the back of his neck deepened. Someone had definitely been through those files. He was particular about the way he left things on his desk. The folders and photographs had been disturbed.

Retrieving a fingerprint kit from the SUV, Nash carefully dusted the folders, the slider and all the other flat surfaces in his office. He doubted the prints he lifted would be useful. Anyone with the skill and smarts to enter his house without breaking the locks wouldn't then become so careless as to leave his or her prints all over everything.

Why *had* someone entered his home? What were

they looking for? Nothing obvious was missing. Not
that he had a houseful of valuables, but why break in
and leave the TV, his laptop and the little cash he kept
in one of the desk drawers?

He went back to the folders and the cave photographs. His mind flashed to the bones on the metal table
and then to Eve's jittery silence after they'd left the lab.
He thought about the car that had swerved toward them
on the side of the road. He couldn't help wondering if
that near miss was somehow connected to the break-in
at his house. To the human remains that had been hidden deep inside a cave for decades.

THE CREAKING FLOORBOARDS catapulted Eve upright on
the bed. She thought at first her mother must have come
home, but Jackie always wore heels to work and they
made a distinct clicking sound on the old parquet floors.
The footsteps Eve heard now were stealthy, as if someone in soft-soled shoes prowled through the darkened
rooms.

She rose quietly and glanced around for a weapon.
Her gun was locked up at home in its usual place beside
her bed. Grabbing a snow globe from the nightstand,
she turned off the lamp and eased across the room to
peer out. A man stood at the end of the narrow hallway, silhouetted by the light filtering in from the street
through the double windows in the den.

He called out, "Hello? Is someone there? Jackie, is
that you?"

Recognizing her ex-stepfather's voice, Eve let out a
relieved breath. "Wayne?"

"Evie?"

She dropped the snow globe to her side and scowled. She hated when anyone but her mother called her Evie. "Yes, it's me."

He gave a low chuckle. "Damn, girl. You scared me half to death."

"I could say the same about you." She came out of the bedroom to confront him. "What are you doing here anyway? You're lucky I didn't bean you with this snow globe."

"I was afraid someone broke in." He walked back a few steps and turned on the hall light. Eve blinked in the sudden brilliance. He gave her a sheepish grin as he held up a pipe wrench. "Looks like we had the same idea."

She reached inside the bedroom doorway and placed the snow globe on the corner of the dresser. Then she turned back expectantly. Wayne Brody and her mother had been divorced for over two decades, having decided after barely a year and a half of marriage that they made better friends than spouses. Eve had nothing against the man. Not anymore. But if she were honest, she'd have to admit she'd never really warmed up to him, maybe because for years she'd harbored the secret hope that her real dad would come back home.

She was a grown woman now and had accepted the reality that Wayne had never been a threat except in her mind. Still, she wasn't particularly comfortable with him coming and going at all hours when her mother wasn't home.

She tried to keep her tone neutral. "You never said what you're doing here."

He toed a metal toolbox on the floor before bending to toss the pipe wrench inside. "Your mom asked me to come over and fix a leaky faucet in the hall bathroom. When I got here, the door was open, but her car wasn't in the driveway. Then I saw a light on at the back of the house and I was afraid someone was inside trying to pick her clean while she was gone." He bent to retrieve the toolbox and place it inside the bathroom door. "What about you?"

Eve bristled at the question despite herself. Why should she have to explain herself to her mother's ex-husband?

She scrutinized him as he busied himself at the faucet. He was in his early fifties, a man of average height, average build, average looks. His hair was light brown, his eyes a nondescript shade of blue. Nothing about Wayne Brody stood out in any way, unlike Eve's father, who had been tall, dark and movie-star handsome. But Gabriel Jareau had left Eve and her mother without a backward glance while Wayne Brody, for all his faults, had stuck around through thick and thin.

"I came by to see Mom," Eve said. "She texted a few minutes ago that she was on her way home. Could we back up for a minute? You said the door was open when you got here. You mean unlocked, don't you?"

He turned in surprise. "No, the kitchen door was wide open like I said."

"But I know I closed it when I came in," Eve insisted.

Wayne thought about it for a moment and then shrugged. "The wind must have blown it open. The latch sometimes won't catch unless you slam the door just right. I've been meaning to fix that, too."

This is not your house. It's not your place to fix my mom's back door. Or her leaky faucet, for that matter. But Eve kept that opinion to herself. Maybe she wasn't as grown-up as she liked to think.

Headlights arced in the driveway and shone through the frosted bathroom window. "That's probably Jackie now." Wayne came out of the bathroom and turned down the hallway toward the kitchen. "You coming?"

"In a minute. I want to have a look around first."

Wayne stopped dead in his tracks and spun. "You still think somebody came in through the back door? You think they could still be in the house?" He sounded a little excited.

"Not really, but I'll feel better if I make certain," Eve said.

"Maybe I should tag along just in case."

"Thanks, Wayne. I've got it covered."

He hesitated for a split second then nodded. "Still hard for me to wrap my head around you being a cop. Seems like yesterday your mom and I were teaching you how to ride a bike."

"Time flies," Eve murmured.

She waited until he'd retreated down the hallway and then went about her search. She didn't expect to find anything. Wayne was probably right about the faulty latch. But the incident on the highway had left her shaken and wary. She wasn't about to take any chances, especially when it came to her mother's safety.

Jackie was just coming through the back door when

Eve returned to the kitchen. Despite the bad weather, her mother looked attractively pulled together in slim black slacks and a green silk blouse that complemented her auburn hair. She wore pearls around her throat and gold hoops in her lobes, all thrifted or bought at the local discount store. Jackie Jareau had a flair for making her bargain-basement wardrobe look like a million dollars, a trait that had not been passed down to her daughter.

Balancing an umbrella in one hand and a grocery bag in the other, she seemed oblivious to the pair in the kitchen.

"Wayne, you here?" she called out as she placed the bag on the mudroom bench and folded the umbrella. Then she kicked off her damp shoes and slid her feet into her favorite fuzzy slippers. "I saw your truck out front. I ordered a pizza on my way home. How's that sound?"

"I'm right here," he said. "Pizza sounds great."

His proximity startled her. She jumped and whirled, glancing from Wayne to Eve and then back again. Her gaze narrowed as she draped her handbag over the back of a bar stool and placed the grocery bag on the counter. "What's going on here? Why are you two staring at me like that?"

Eve moved up to the bar. "Nothing's going on. We were just waiting for you. You didn't tell me Wayne would be here."

"Didn't I? Must have slipped my mind." She removed the items from the grocery bag and began storing them in the pantry.

Wayne leaned a shoulder against the doorway and folded his arms as he watched his ex-wife move about the kitchen. His blue gaze seemed to take in her every move. "You missed all the excitement. Your daughter nearly knocked me in the head with one of your snow globes."

Eve tamped down her annoyance at his dramatics. "And you armed yourself with a pipe wrench. We both thought someone had broken in," she explained to her mother.

Jackie glanced over her shoulder, puzzled. "Why on earth would you think that? I've never had any concern here."

"Don't be lulled into a false sense of security," Eve said. "Crime is on the rise all over town."

Jackie sighed. "My daughter, the police detective."

"She's right," Wayne said. "You can't be too careful these days."

"I appreciate your concern, both of you, but I'm not about to live my life in fear."

"No one said anything about living in fear, Mom. Just be careful, okay? Especially when you get home this late."

Jackie turned from the pantry with a worried frown. "This is a very puzzling conversation. Why do I get the feeling you're not telling me everything? Has something happened that I should know about?"

An icy breeze blew down Eve's neck. All the doors and windows were closed so she wanted to assume the air conditioner had kicked on.

"Well?" Jackie pressed.

"Nothing's happened. I'm just asking you to be careful, that's all." Eve could feel Wayne's gaze on her now. Why did the man's presence irritate her so much? No reason to begrudge their friendship. He was a good guy who would do anything for her mother. A dutiful daughter should be grateful for that.

Jackie gave her a long look. Then she came over and tipped Eve's face toward the light. "How did that happen?"

Eve's fingers went to the tenderness on her cheek. "I slipped and fell. It's nothing. Just a scrape."

Jackie's gaze darkened. "How did you fall?"

"It's nothing," Eve insisted.

"Did you put something on it?"

"Yes, ma'am. Just the way you taught me."

Her mother was far from appeased. "I know there's more to the story. I can see it in your eyes."

Eve sighed. "Chief Bowden and I had a flat tire on our way back from Tallahassee. I slipped on the wet shoulder and tumbled down an embankment. That's the truth." *More or less.*

"What were you doing in Tallahassee?" Wayne asked.

He remained in the doorway with his shoulder against the frame, but the subtle tension in his voice belied his casual stance. His eyes seemed a little too piercing, his whole countenance frozen and unnatural.

That strange breeze whispered against Eve's neck like a ghostly caress.

Watch your back, Boo.

Chapter Three

Jackie didn't seem to notice the sudden crackle of electricity in the air. She grabbed a bottle of wine from the rack on the counter and then rummaged in a drawer for a corkscrew. "I don't know about you two, but I could use a drink. All this scare talk has put me on edge. Let's have a nice glass of wine and try to relax before dinner gets here."

Wayne straightened from the doorway. "None for me. I'd better get to that leaky faucet or I'll be here all night."

Jackie gave him an appreciative smile. "Thanks, Wayne. You're a lifesaver."

"I'm always happy to help. You know that."

"I do know." They exchanged an intimate glance.

Wayne disappeared back into the house and Eve stared after him as she plopped down at the bar. "Do you think it's a good idea to have him over here so often to fix things?"

Jackie leaned against the bar, cupping her wineglass in one hand. "You heard him. He's happy to help out."

"I'm sure he is, but maybe you should call a plumber

or professional handyman now and then. Or even let me have a go at it."

"Why would I spend good money on a plumber when Wayne is just down the street?"

Eve sighed and shook her head helplessly. "Come on, Mom. You'd have to be blind not to notice the way he looks at you."

Jackie seemed genuinely taken aback. "What on earth are you talking about?"

"The man still has feelings for you. Don't tell me you haven't figured that out yet." Eve reached for the wine bottle.

"Oh, good grief, Wayne doesn't have *romantic* feelings for me." Jackie gave a little bark of laughter. "That's crazy. We've been divorced for over twenty years."

"Yet he still lives right down the street from you. He comes running whenever you call." Eve poured herself a glass of wine. "There's no time limit on how long someone can carry a torch."

"You should know," Jackie muttered.

"What?"

"Nothing." Her mother was silent for a moment as she searched Eve's face. "Where is this coming from?"

Eve shrugged. "It's something I've thought for a while."

"Then why wait until now to bring it up?"

"Because I do realize it's none of my business," Eve said with a wry smile.

"No, it isn't," her mother agreed bluntly. "But let me clarify something for you anyway. Wayne and I go back a long way. We were friends before we got married and we've remained friends since the divorce. That's not going to change. We like and respect one another. We enjoy each other's company. There's nothing more to our relationship than that."

"Maybe not for you," Eve muttered.

Jackie's mouth tightened. "All right, that's enough. I know how you feel about Wayne. You've never even bothered to pretend. It was understandable when you were a child, but you're an adult now. It's time you start tending to your own life."

Eve grew defensive. "I do tend to my own life."

"Not that I can see. When was the last time you had a real date? Let me tell you something, Evie. Time flies by faster than you think."

"I know that."

Jackie gave her a sage look. "I hope you do. But something tells me you didn't come over to talk about either of our love lives. You certainly didn't come here to talk about my ex-husband."

"I didn't come to talk about Wayne, no. I want to ask you about Daddy."

Something flickered in Jackie's eyes before she glanced away. "What about him?"

"He sent money to you after he left, didn't he? How long did that go on?"

A bitter edge crept into her mother's voice. "Not long enough, but it hardly matters now, does it?"

Eve shrugged. "It matters to me. How long? A few weeks…a few months?"

"I don't know. I can't remember things that happened last week, let alone three decades ago."

"Try, Mom."

She sighed. "At first, he sent money home almost every week. Then it dwindled to once a month and then to nothing at all. That went on for a couple of months, the best I remember."

"Cash, checks, money orders?"

"Always cash. I thought he was crazy for trusting the post office, but Gabriel never did have a lick of common sense when it came to money."

"Did he include a letter or note?"

"Sometimes."

"What did he say?"

"I don't remember every word."

"Just the gist," Eve coaxed.

Jackie closed her eyes on another deep sigh. "Let me think. He talked about work sometimes and about where he was headed next. Mostly he talked about you."

Eve felt a strange flutter in the pit of her stomach. "What about me?"

"How much he loved and missed you. How sorry he was that he couldn't be with you. That sort of thing."

And yet he'd apparently abandoned her without a backward glance. "Do you still have those letters?"

"Why would I keep them?" Jackie topped off her wineglass. Was that a slight tremor in her hand or merely Eve's imagination? "I got rid of all that stuff years ago."

"What about the postcards he sent to me?"

Her mother's shrug seemed nonchalant, but Eve noticed how carefully she still avoided eye contact. "You used to have them pinned to the bulletin board in your room. I haven't seen them in a long time, so I figured you'd either thrown them out when you left for college or took them with you."

"Did Daddy ever mention coming back home?" Eve tried to keep the wistful tone from her voice, but Jackie heard something that caused her frown to deepen.

"He made it pretty clear the night he left that he wasn't coming back."

"Did the two of you argue?"

"We always argued."

"Strange," Eve murmured. "I didn't hear you that night. Sometimes I would."

"We should never have let that happen. Not that this excuses anything, but we were so young and both of us had quick tempers." Her mother's eyes glittered. "No one has ever been able to push my buttons the way Gabriel Jareau did."

"Do you think it's possible he came back to Black Creek without you knowing?"

"I guess it's possible, but he would have tried to see you if he'd come back. Whatever our problems, he loved you, Evie." Jackie's expression softened. "You should never doubt that."

"And yet he left me."

"He left both of us."

At the back of Eve's mind, she could see her father climbing into that unfamiliar car with the platinum blonde behind the wheel and the mysterious man looking out the window in the back seat.

"Mom?"

Jackie seemed to rouse from a deep reverie. "Hmm?"

"I overheard you tell someone once that he left you for another woman. Do you know who she was?"

Her mother's hand crept to her throat. "You heard that? Oh, honey, I'm sorry. I never meant for you to know."

"No need to be sorry. Like you said, it was a long time ago."

Jackie shook her head in regret. "You overheard that conversation and all this time, you never said a word."

"I didn't want to believe it."

"Of course not. You always adored your daddy. You thought the sun rose and set on that man. And he, you."

Eve swallowed. "So did you ever try to find out who she was?"

"No, I never did." Her mother glanced up. "This may sound harsh, but after a while, I really didn't care who she was or where they'd gone off to. I didn't have time to care. I had a child to raise, a mortgage and bills to pay. So many more important things to worry about than the identity of my husband's girlfriend."

But even after all these years, she couldn't quite keep the edge of resentment from her voice. She couldn't quite stifle the faraway look in her eyes when she mentioned her first husband's name.

Eve nodded. "I understand. Do you think she was someone from Black Creek? I mean, you must have heard talk, right? No one can keep a secret in this town." Yet John Doe's bones had remained hidden for decades.

Jackie picked up a towel and idly wiped a ring from the counter. "Why all these questions? He left so long ago. What difference does any of this make now?"

"Surely you can understand why I'm curious," Eve said. "He was my father and I remember so little about him. It's not the first time I've asked about him."

"No, but you haven't brought him up in a long time. I'd hoped you'd moved on as I have."

Have you, though? If you're so indifferent, why do you avoid talking about him? Why did you throw all of his things away when you knew I might someday want them?

"Just one more question," Eve said. "Was he ever involved in a car accident?"

Jackie had been lifting her drink, but now she paused with the glass in midair. "He had a motorcycle wreck the year you were born. I'm sure I've mentioned it before."

"I don't think so. If you did, I've forgotten. How severe were his injuries?"

"He was in pretty bad shape. Why?"

"Did he break his right arm? His right leg? His left ankle?"

The wineglass exploded in Jackie's hand and her face went deathly white. Red wine spilled over her fingers, mixing with the blood that gushed from a cut in her palm as the crystal crashed against the tile floor.

Eve jumped up and hurried around the bar. "Mom, you're bleeding. Here, let me see." She pulled her mother toward the sink.

Jackie seemed stunned. "I don't know what happened," she mumbled. "The glass just shattered in my hand."

Wayne appeared in the doorway. "I heard glass breaking. Everything okay in here?"

Eve glanced over her shoulder. How had he appeared in the doorway so quickly? Had he been eavesdropping on their conversation?

"Mom cut her hand."

"What? How?"

"A glass broke."

He avoided the shards on the floor as he rushed to the sink. "How bad is it?"

"It's nothing," Jackie insisted. But sweat beaded at her temples as she slumped against the sink, looking as if she might pass out at any second.

"Mom, you okay? Do you need to sit down?"

Wayne gently took her hand. "Let me have a look first." Eve put her arm around her mother's waist for support while he washed the cut under running water. The blood kept oozing. He wrapped her hand in a clean dish towel. "We'd better get you to the ER. Looks like you need stitches."

Jackie started to protest, but Eve quickly agreed. "He's right. It's deep and you may have glass slivers inside the cut that could cause infection."

"I'm parked right out front." Wayne ushered Jackie toward the door before Eve could protest. She tried not to resent his tendency to take over. Her petty grievances couldn't matter less now. The faster her mother got to the ER, the better. And Wayne's vehicle happened to be handy.

He glanced back. "Can you take care of things here?"

"Yes, of course. Just keep me posted."

She watched from the window until Wayne's truck pulled away from the curb and then she cleaned up the mess on the floor and carried the glass fragments out to the trash. After that, she killed a bit of time checking her messages and email before heading back down the hallway to her old bedroom. She sat down at her desk and removed the top drawer so that she could retrieve the envelope she'd long ago taped to the back. Surprisingly, her mother had never found her hiding place. Or if she had, she'd never said anything.

Peeling off the tape, Eve opened the envelope and dumped her father's postcards on top of the desk. There were only three—two from New Orleans and one from San Antonio. Those postcards and the dime she wore around her neck were all she had left of him.

Eve arranged the cards in chronological order according to the postmarks. The messages were brief and she knew them all by heart. *Miss you, Boo. Wish you were here, Boo. Be a good girl for your mama, Boo.*

Maybe it was Eve's imagination, but she noticed something now that had escaped her as a child. The handwriting on the San Antonio postcard looked subtly different from the two New Orleans postcards. She dug around in the drawer for a magnifying glass but couldn't find one.

Tension knotted her shoulders. She returned the postcards to the envelope and carried it with her into the kitchen. Perching at the bar, she massaged her sore muscles while she waited to hear from her mother.

NASH WAS STILL seated behind his desk when his cell phone rang. He automatically checked the screen before he answered. *Unknown Caller.*

His first thought was that Grace had somehow finagled the use of a phone, and he was in no mood to deal with his ex-wife tonight. He didn't want to listen to her excuses, or worse, her accusations. Nash never wanted to hear from her again, but that wasn't a realistic desire considering her nature and the fact that her trial would be starting soon.

Best-case scenario for him, her attorney would request a change of venue and then his department wouldn't be charged with escorting her to and from county lockup every day. He'd still see her in court, though. No getting around that.

The phone buzzed persistently. His gut instinct was to let the call go to voice mail, but as chief of police, he was never really off duty. He hit the accept button with a grimace and lifted the phone to his ear.

"Nash Bowden."

The caller remained silent, but Nash could hear music and laughter in the background.

"Hello? Anyone there?"

"You need to leave them bones alone," a gruff voice informed him.

"What?"

"You heard me," the woman said in a hushed tone. "Leave 'em be if you know what's good for you."

Not Grace, obviously. Nash tried to place the caller. She sounded older, at least fifty, with the grit of smoke and hard living around the edges.

He was instantly on alert and intrigued. "Who is this?"

"My name's not important. You don't know me. And

don't bother trying to track me down. I'm throwing this phone away as soon as we're done."

So she was using a burner, which implied a certain amount of technical sophistication. Disposable phones could be traced, but not easily and not with the limited resources available to Nash's department.

"Your name matters a great deal if you're trying to interfere in an official police investigation," he informed her. "I need to know who you are and the reason you're making this call."

A slight hesitation. "You don't think what happened out on the highway tonight is reason enough for me to call you?"

He put the phone on speaker and placed it on his desk, then reached for pen and paper to take notes. "What happened on the highway tonight?"

"You should know. You were there."

An icy finger traced along his spine. "Were you driving the car that sideswiped my vehicle?"

"No, sir, I was not."

"Were you a passenger?"

Another pause. "That's not important, either."

"Are you saying what happened tonight wasn't an accident?" Nash pressed.

"I'm saying next time there won't be a close call."

"Is that a threat?"

"Call it a warning."

Nash scowled down at the paper. "What do you know about the remains that were found in McNally's Cave?"

"I know it's best to let the dead rest in peace."

"Do you know the deceased's name and how he came to be down in that cave? Do you know who killed him?"

He heard the sharp intake of her breath. "Lord, mister. Did you hear what I said? Leave 'em be. You have no idea what you're dealing with. *Who* you're dealing with."

"Then why don't you tell me?"

"I've said too much already."

"You haven't told me anything. Wait—"

The connection dropped, leaving Nash with nothing but a blank piece of paper and a dozen questions swirling in his head. He swore aloud, the four-letter expletive echoing unpleasantly in the silent room.

According to the female caller, the incident on the highway had been deliberate. The driver had purposefully swerved toward them, but why? If Eve hadn't lost her footing at that precise moment, the evening might have gone very differently. He didn't want to think about how close he'd come to losing her forever, but now he could think of nothing else.

Outside, the wind had picked up. Nash could hear the faint squeak of the garden gate as it swung back and forth in the breeze. Odd because he never left that gate unlatched. He'd checked it earlier, hadn't he? Or had he overlooked it in his haste to search the garden?

For the second time that evening, he removed his weapon from the desk drawer and went back out into the night. The ruffling leaves sounded like rain, and he could hear the tinkle of wind chimes in his neighbor's backyard. The moon cast a soft glow over the brick pathway he followed across the yard to the gate.

The wrought iron clanged rhythmically in the breeze.

Keeping to the shadows, Nash peered through the metal rods into the side yard and out to the street. Oily puddles glistened beneath the streetlights. The night had deepened since his earlier search and an eerie hush seemed to fall over the landscape.

He opened the gate and stepped through. Pressing a shoulder against the side of the house, he eased through the darkness to the front yard. He didn't think he could be seen from the street, but someone must have been watching for him. Two houses down, headlights came on, the dual beams sweeping over him as an old pickup truck sputtered to life, and the driver U-turned and sped away.

Nash bolted across the yard and down the sidewalk, but the truck easily outpaced him. The driver turned on squealing tires at the next intersection and the vehicle was soon out of sight.

Nash stared down the street in frustration. It was useless to pursue on foot, and by the time he sprinted back home for the SUV or even called for a patrol car, the truck would be long gone.

Searching the night for a moment longer, he turned and strode back to his house. As he headed up the walkway, his phone rang again. *Unknown Caller* flashed on his screen.

He accepted the call and lifted the phone to his ear as he stepped back through the gate.

"You've been warned," the same gruff voice informed him. She sounded out of breath this time, as if she'd just run back to her truck. "Don't say you weren't."

Chapter Four

Despite her late night, Eve clocked in an hour early the next morning. She'd waited anxiously to hear from her mother before heading home the evening before. Jackie had called from the emergency room around eleven, insisting that, except for a few stitches, she was none the worse for wear. As soon as she got home, she took a pain pill and went straight to bed. Wayne had offered to stay over in case she needed anything, but Jackie had sent him on his way, insisting she'd had enough of his hovering for one night. Nor was she in the mood for any more of Eve's questions. Fair enough. She'd been through a lot and for now Eve decided it was best not to press her mother on the issue.

She'd walked home in the dark with her father's postcards safely tucked inside her bag, still pondering her mother's accident. How could a wineglass shatter in one's hand like that? It was almost as if her mother had unwittingly applied undue pressure to the fragile sides in distress, but why would Eve's questions prompt such a strong reaction? Why *now*?

Back at home, she'd stayed up until well past midnight studying the handwriting on the postcards. Her vision blurring from exhaustion and intense concentration, she'd finally convinced herself she had imagined the discrepancies. Did she really think someone had forged her father's handwriting in order to convince his estranged wife and five-year-old daughter that he was still alive?

Daylight had brought a clearer head and a mile-long list of things she needed to accomplish. She was deep into the musty-smelling missing-persons files when Nash stopped by her desk. She saw him approach out of the corner of her eye, but she pretended not to notice until he spoke.

"Good morning, Detective Jareau."

"Morning, Chief. You're here bright and early."

"So are you. No ill effects from that tumble you took last night?"

"I'm fine," she assured him.

He examined the scrape on her cheek and nodded. "Good. We've got a lot of ground to cover today."

Outwardly, Eve remained calm and collected, but as always in his presence, she felt an unsettling stir of butterflies in her stomach. After six years, her feelings for Nash Bowden should have long since withered and died, but somehow her attraction had only grown stronger.

When she'd first joined the Black Creek Police Department fresh out of the Florida Law Enforcement Academy, she'd heard the gossip about his troubled marriage and subsequent separation. Those rumors and the haunted look in his eyes—not to mention her rookie status—had convinced her the police chief was off-limits, especially to her.

But every once in a while she would catch him looking at her when no one else was around and the *way* he looked at her... She was only human. She'd slipped once and made the first move after a particularly harrowing arrest. They were alone after the danger had passed and she'd let adrenaline and her emotions get the best of her. Nash had kissed her back, not politely or tentatively, but with the pent-up passion of a drowning man.

The intensity of that kiss had persuaded Eve more than anything else that the Black Creek chief of police was a dangerous man for a woman like her. She wasn't naive. A man who kissed the way he did might require far more from a partner than Eve was willing to give.

Not that any of that mattered these days. Nash had kept his distance after that kiss and she'd kept hers.

But now here he was, seeking her out yet again. His expression seemed all business so she tried not to wonder if his feelings had secretly lingered the way hers had. She tried not to think about what might have happened if she'd kissed him again that night. Kissed him the way he needed to be kissed.

She gave him a brief perusal, allowing her gaze to explore for only a split second before returning her attention to the file. He wore his typical uniform of jeans, casual shirt and boots. Eve was dressed much the same, having retired her uniform (except on formal or ceremonial occasions) when she made detective three years ago on her thirtieth birthday. She'd celebrated with a few friends and colleagues at a local bar, keeping one eye on the door in case Nash decided to join them. He hadn't. She'd gone home that night both intensely relieved and bitterly disappointed.

A few months later, news had spread through the grapevine that his divorce had been finalized. By then, Eve had been involved with a man she'd known from high school. Nice guy. Funny. Kind. Easy on the eyes. They should have made a good match, but her reticence to commit had eventually doomed the relationship.

So here *she* was, still nursing unrequited feelings for her superior. Funny how things worked out. Now that she and Nash were finally free to be together, they'd never been further apart.

She closed the file and folded her hands on the desk, allowing a hint of excitement to creep into her voice. "Does this mean we're a go?"

He looked momentarily startled, as if his thoughts had uncomfortably meshed with hers. "I'm sorry?"

"You said we had a lot of ground to cover today. I assumed that meant you'd contacted Mr. McNally about going down in the cave." Eve waited a beat. "The equipment and backup have all been arranged. I just need to know the day and time."

Something seemed to click at the back of his mind and he nodded absently. "The cave. Right. We'll get to that. Probably a good idea to wait a day or two in case any of the passageways flooded during the storm."

A day or two? Eve needed answers now. "I'd like to go down today if at all possible."

He perched a hip on the edge of her desk and gave her one of those hooded looks, the kind that made her momentarily forget their surroundings and circumstances. "What's the hurry? The remains were buried in that cavern for decades and they aren't going anywhere. Another day or two won't matter."

It matters to me.

"Besides, the delay will give Dr. Forester enough time to complete her analysis," he added.

"Okay."

He cocked his head at her obvious disappointment. "I know you're anxious to get down in that cave, but as I said yesterday, those tunnels are dangerous in the best times. We're not going to take any chances."

She nodded. "It's your call."

"Anyway, we have a more pressing issue this morning," he informed her. "It may be connected to the same case."

That got her attention. "What are you talking about?"

"We've got a lead on the vehicle that sideswiped us last night."

She sat up straighter, her heart thudding in trepidation. "How is that connected to the John Doe case?"

He stood. "Come on. I'll explain everything on the way."

Eve rose, too. "Where are we going? Wait," she said impatiently when he moved away from her desk. "How were you able to get a lead on that vehicle with just the first two letters of the license plate number?"

He turned back. "There's only one registration in our area that matches those two numbers and the vehicle description. The sedan belongs to a man named Ron Naples. Do you know him?"

Eve rolled the name around in her memory banks and then shook her head. "The name doesn't ring any bells. Should I know him?"

"No, but I thought I'd ask since you've lived here all your life. He's seventy-eight years old, lives out near Myrtle Cove. You and I are going to drive out there this morning and have a chat with him."

Eve bit her lip in contemplation as she came around her desk. "His age could explain the erratic driving. Like you said, he may have been distracted or disoriented by the flashing lights. Or there could be a medical problem." She paused. "But none of that explains why you think he's connected to John Doe."

"It involves an anonymous phone call I received last night. The sooner we get on the road, the sooner I can explain everything. You coming?" He didn't wait for her answer, but instead turned and strode down the corridor to the back entrance.

Wild horses couldn't keep me away, Eve thought as she hurried to catch up. She tried to ignore the knot in her chest and the warning shiver up her backbone. *This is just a case like any other.* But she knew better. Fingering the dime beneath her shirt, she followed Nash outside.

The day was already hot and steamy. She paused for a split second to scan the sky. Not a storm cloud in sight. Not the kind she could see anyway.

Her gaze rested on the damaged side of Nash's SUV. The ugly scrapes and dents reminded her all too vividly of that split second of panic when the car's headlights had blinded her, freezing her to the spot like a trapped deer.

She went around to the other side and climbed in. "So don't keep me in suspense," she prompted as Nash started the engine. "Tell me about this anonymous phone call."

He nodded as he slipped on his sunglasses. She could no longer read his eyes, but his mouth was set in a thin line. "Someone using a burner phone called my cell last night. The caller was female. Raspy voice, country accent. Older, I'm guessing, but not elderly. She refused to give me her name."

"How do you think she got your number?"

"I'm still trying to figure that out. The dispatchers don't give out my cell number and I can't imagine Tess ever letting it slip."

No, his administrative assistant was as loyal and discreet as they came. "What did the caller want?" Eve asked.

"She said we should leave the bones alone."

"You think she was referring to John Doe?"

"We haven't recovered any other bones that I'm aware of." He paused briefly to look both ways before pulling out of the gated parking lot onto the street.

Eve wiped her palms on the tops of her thighs. Was it possible the anonymous caller was the platinum blonde she'd seen in the car the night her father went away? His companion would certainly be older, at least in her late forties or early fifties, but it seemed a stretch to think it could be the same woman after all these years. However, if Gabriel Jareau had been murdered, the other two people in the car that night might know something. Who were they and where had they been living since that fateful night?

For years, Eve had sought to understand her father's abandonment. How could a man she'd loved and adored walk away from his wife and child without a backward glance? Now that those answers might be coming to the surface, Eve wanted nothing so much as to turn back the clock to the day before those unidentified remains had been found in McNally's Cave. Before her mother had broken that glass in distress. Before old doubts had once again started to niggle.

"You okay?"

She roused from her reverie with a slight jerk. "What? Yes, I'm fine. Why?"

Nash turned his head to study her for a moment. "You seemed a million miles away. You've been distracted ever since we left the lab yesterday. What's going on, Eve?"

The butterflies stirred again at the way he said her name. Softly. Intimately. Or was that merely wishful thinking?

She stared straight ahead and tried to sound normal. "It's this case. I know you said John Doe isn't a priority, but I can't stop thinking about it. And now that I know about the anonymous phone call, I'm more determined than ever to find out what happened down in that cave."

His voice lowered. "Are you sure that's all it is?"

"Of course. What else would it be?"

He seemed on the verge of saying something else, then turned back to the road. "Maybe I'm a little over-sensitive these days. I'm well aware of all the stares and whispers. People I've known for years have been avoiding me like the plague ever since Grace's arrest."

Eve felt outraged on his behalf, but she merely shrugged. "Ignore them. People in this town like to talk. They'll move on to something else in a few days."

"You don't ever wonder?"

"Wonder what?" she asked carefully.

"If I knew and covered for her."

Eve answered without hesitation. "Not for one second. You would never do that, especially when a child was involved. Besides, you were there when she was apprehended. If you'd wanted to warn her away or help her escape, you could have easily done so."

He said nothing to that even though Eve had the strangest feeling he wanted to open up. *Confession is good for the soul*, she started to remind him, but that would be extremely hypocritical considering the secret she now kept from him.

"What else did the caller say to you?" she asked.

"She implied the hit-and-run wasn't an accident. That the car deliberately swerved toward us last night."

Eve's fingers curled around the edge of the seat. "She admitted that? She actually tried to run us down."

"She claimed she wasn't the driver. She wouldn't admit to being a passenger, either, but she knew all about the incident. If she's right, I can only assume we were followed from the lab. Sure makes the timing of that flat tire suspect."

"Doesn't it, though?" Eve hesitated, her gaze fiercely focused on the road. Time for a small confession of her own. "I saw someone in the parking lot when I came out of the lab last night. The dome light was on in his car. He turned it off when he saw me. I could have sworn—" She broke off.

Nash shot her a glance. "What?"

She shook her head. "It just seemed strange that he turned the light off as soon as he saw me."

"Do you think he was waiting for us?"

"Maybe. He was sitting alone in a dark sedan when I noticed him."

Nash's voice sharpened. "Why didn't you mention this last night?"

"I didn't think much of it at the time. I figured he was waiting to pick someone up from work. Then everything happened so fast on the highway…" She shook her head, as if trying to clear away cobwebs from her memory. "Even now, I can't swear it was the same car. There are hundreds of vehicles on the road matching that description. But now that I know about the phone call, I'm finding it a little hard to chalk up the two incidents to coincidence."

"That phone call changes everything," Nash agreed. "Our cold case has suddenly become red-hot."

Eve STUDIED THE passing scenery in quiet contemplation. The buildings grew sparse as they approached the edge of town. Nothing out that way but a few scattered convenience stores with gas pumps, an automotive garage and an old church on one corner, the weathered spires rising up through a canopy of pecan trees.

Her mother had taken her to that church on Easter

Sunday once. Eve could still remember the way Jackie's pretty floral dress had swirled around her slender legs, giving the dreamy illusion that she could float. Eve had hunted Easter eggs with dozens of other children that day, and afterward, they'd met her father for lunch at the diner. Eve had sat on his knee and helped herself to his root beer float. They'd seemed like a normal, happy family, but when she looked back, she had vague recollections of something she didn't understand simmering beneath the surface.

She tucked her hair behind her ears as she glanced at Nash. "Anything else I should know about that phone call?" she asked in dread.

"The woman said we'd been warned."

"Warned," Eve repeated numbly. Her thoughts raced as images flashed in her head. The strange car at the curb. The platinum blonde behind the wheel and the sinister man in the back seat. Her father's last goodbye.

What had that trio been up to the night Gabriel Jareau left town?

The lucky dime suddenly felt cold and ominous against her skin.

"There's something else you should know," Nash said. "Someone was in my house while I was gone. The slider in my office was open when I got home, but I couldn't find any sign of a break-in. No tool marks or broken glass. Nothing. I don't know how they got in."

"What was taken?"

He shrugged. "That's just it. Nothing seems to be missing. There was cash in a drawer and they left it.

Didn't touch the laptop or TV. But I'm pretty sure they went through the folders on my desk."

"What do you think they were looking for?"

"I can only guess. I kept a physical copy of the John Doe file at home. The photographs from the excavation site were out of order. I know because I tend to keep things a certain way."

Why did he have a copy of the John Doe file at home? Eve wondered. Did he not trust her to work the case?

"I know what you're thinking," he said.

"I'm not thinking anything, just listening."

"You're probably wondering if I intend to meddle in your investigation every step of the way, but that's not it. You're right. There's something about this case that grabs you and won't let go. I have a bad feeling there's more to it than an old homicide. I keep returning to that file and studying those images because something is nagging at me, like I'm missing something important." He paused on a grimace. "Does that sound as ridiculous as I think it does?"

"No, because I have the same feeling."

He frowned at the road. "I'm thinking we should work together on this one. Hear me out," he said before she could protest. "You'll still take lead, but I'd like to be involved in the investigation if that's okay with you."

Eve could hardly argue. "You're the boss."

"I'm not trying to pull rank, but this one has become a little personal for me. Right after I received the anonymous phone call, I saw an old pickup truck parked down the street from my place. As soon as I noticed the vehicle, the driver U-turned and sped away.

That's when the woman called a second time to tell me I'd been warned."

"You think she was in the truck?"

"That's the impression I got."

"So she's watching your house."

"Apparently she was last night."

Why Nash's house and not hers? Eve thought. Did he have a connection to the case she didn't know about? Or was guilt and paranoia making her suspicious of his motives?

"Here's another question," she said. "Assuming your tire was sabotaged and we were followed from the lab, how did that person know we'd be in Tallahassee in the first place? I didn't mention our trip to anyone, did you?"

"Tess keeps my schedule and she always knows how to reach me, but she also knows to be discreet. If someone had called asking questions about my whereabouts, she would have been alarmed enough to try to get a name and number, and then she would have notified me immediately."

"So maybe our suspect followed us *to* the lab and waited in the parking lot for us to leave. Maybe someone has been keeping tabs on our movements ever since the remains were dug up."

He nodded. "Your mysterious man in the dark sedan."

"Or your anonymous female caller. Or both."

"We've got ourselves a real puzzle, don't we?" She heard her own excitement mirrored in his voice as he flashed her a grin, momentarily lightening the mood.

She shrugged and answered with a reluctant smile, keeping things casual. But her pulse thudded as their gazes lingered for a split second. He turned back to the road and she turned back to the passing scenery.

They fell silent again, each lost in thought. Something had occurred to Eve as she stared out the window, but she was hesitant to bring up the subject of Nash's ex-wife. Grace Bowden was a tricky subject for more reasons than one.

"What is it?" he asked.

She turned. "What do you mean?"

"You're thinking hard about something. I can almost hear the gears turning. What's going on inside that head of yours?"

Eve averted her gaze, refocusing her attention on a tiny chip in the windshield. "Actually, I was thinking about Grace."

"What about her?" His tone hardened almost infinitesimally.

Eve braced herself. "Would you mind if I go see her?"

The silence seemed charged all of a sudden, like summer air before a lightning storm. "Why do you want to see her? I don't see the point."

"At the time of her arrest, she said she'd known about the grave in the cavern since she was a little girl. She thought Maya Lamb was buried there." Maya had been the first child to go missing, twenty-eight years before Kylie Buchanan.

Nash lifted a hand from the steering wheel and rubbed the back of his neck, a habit when he was either tired or stressed, or both. "Grace said a lot of things at the time of her arrest. She's not the most reliable narrator of her own story."

"You don't believe she knew about that grave?"

He dropped his hand back to the steering wheel. "Whether she knew or not, she was just a little girl when all that went down. She couldn't have had anything to do with John Doe's murder."

"Of course not. But maybe she wasn't the only one who visited that grave. She said as a child she spent a lot of time exploring McNally's Cave. Maybe she encountered someone else down there at some point."

"The killer returning to the scene of the crime?"

"It does happen," Eve insisted. "I know it's a long shot, but I'd still like to talk to her. Assuming she would agree to see me." Eve paused, trying to analyze his reaction from her periphery. "I'll be respectful. And I'll do my best not to say or do anything that will upset her."

"I'm not concerned about that. It's you I'm worried about."

"Me?" she said in surprise. "I'll be fine."

"You might not sound so confident if you knew her the way I do." He glanced in the rearview mirror as if fearful his ex-wife might have slipped up behind them. "She can come across shy and reserved with strangers, but underneath she's clever and manipulative. The most unrepentant person I've ever known, and that's saying something in our line of work. She isn't at all sorry she took that child. She's only sorry she didn't get away with it."

And yet you married her. Eve bit her lip and nodded. "I'll be careful."

He turned to scrutinize her. "Doesn't matter how careful you are. She'll still find a way to get under your skin and you won't even see it coming."

"If you're that concerned, come with me."

His mouth tightened and she could see the throb of a muscle in his jaw. "I'd rather not."

Was he worried Grace might still be able to get under *his* skin? Was it possible, after everything that had happened, he still had feelings for his ex-wife?

"I understand," Eve said. "Maybe it's for the best that I go alone anyway. She might feel more comfortable opening up to a stranger. If and when she agrees to see me, I'll let you know."

"This is a bad idea," he warned.

She drew a breath, determined to stick to her guns. "Maybe. But if you're really serious about letting me take lead on this case, then I need to do things my way. Grace may know something and not even realize it."

"I won't try to stop you," he said. "But when you're with her, you need to watch what you say and how you say it. Don't let her get inside your head. Don't let things get personal. And whatever you do, don't turn your back on that woman."

Chapter Five

They traveled the rest of the way in awkward silence. As they neared their destination, Eve finally turned away from the side window to study Nash's profile. At the mention of his ex-wife, he'd fallen into a deep funk. She didn't blame him. She could only imagine what must have gone through his head the moment he realized the woman he'd once loved was the suspect for whom he and the FBI had been searching for days.

She strove to relieve the tension by circling back to the subject of Ron Naples. "Can you tell me anything else about him? Do you know if he has family in the area?"

"I haven't had time to run a full background check," Nash said in a clipped, cool tone. "You know as much as I do."

"Do you at least know if he lives alone? We should be prepared for what we may walk into."

"We'll find out soon enough. You've got your sidearm?"

She tapped her holster. "Of course."

"Just keep your eyes and ears open. I'm not expecting

trouble, but you never know. I wasn't expecting trouble last night and look what happened." He stopped for an oncoming vehicle and then made a left turn off the highway, heading deeper into the countryside.

"Could have been worse," Eve said.

He nodded, his expression grim. "Now that the adrenaline has faded and you've had time to think back through everything, have you remembered anything else about the vehicle you saw in the parking lot? Partial plate number, any dents or scratches that you noticed?"

"It was dark and raining. If the interior light hadn't been on, I would never have noticed it at all."

"What about the man inside? Can you describe him?"

She thought back, but all she saw in her mind's eye was the nebulous silhouette of the man in the back seat.

"He appeared to be alone. That's the only thing that comes to mind."

"Old, young, thin, heavyset?" Nash prompted.

"I didn't get a good look. I was distracted and the light was only on for a moment after I first saw him." She closed her eyes, focusing her mind on the interior of the car before the light had gone out. "Okay, maybe I do remember something. It's nothing concrete, but I have the impression he was middle-aged or a little older. Fifties, maybe. Average build."

Nash nodded. "That's good. What about hair color?"

"Brown, I think."

"See? We always remember more than we think we do. Just relax and let it all come back to you. What else?"

He put a finger to his lips to silence me. Had he,

though? Or had that been a projection brought on by a twenty-eight-year-old memory?

Like Grace Bowden, Eve was an unreliable narrator of her story. So many years had passed since that final night with her father, and yet her memory of his departure was as clear as though it had happened yesterday. But that in itself was suspect. She'd only been five years old when he left. How could she have such a vivid memory of that night? Had she really witnessed him get into a car with two strangers or had everything been a dream brought on by the trauma of his departure?

The woods crowded in on them as they headed north toward the river. Spanish moss hung in thick sheets from the live oaks, and kudzu crept like a dark green shadow up dead tree trunks and over the rooftops of abandoned houses. The landscape was primal and menacing, the air heavy with the dank smell of the swamp.

All along the river, new homes had cropped up alongside prewar bungalows perched on stilts. Ron Naples's home was one of the latter, though the house and yard looked immaculate. A screen porch wrapped around the entire structure, allowing unobstructed views of the water, the woods and the road. No one was about. No vehicles in the driveway. No twitching curtains or barking dogs. The silence seemed eerie and oppressive. Eve suppressed a shiver as she got out of the vehicle and circled around to Nash's side.

"I haven't been out this way in a long time," she said. "It's like being miles from anywhere."

"If you ignore all the new houses," Nash said dryly.

"Yes, there is that. I'd forgotten how the river smells. It's a scent like no other." Her father used to bring her to a spot not far from there to fish. Mostly she'd picked blackberries while he kept an eye on their poles. Or had she imagined that, too?

Eve brushed a mosquito from her eyelashes. "We'll be eaten alive out here."

Nash opened his door and dug around for a can of insect repellant. They both sprayed themselves down.

"Place looks deserted," Eve said as they started across the yard. "Should I go around back while you take the front?"

"Let's see if anyone answers the door first."

Eve nodded and walked up the steps, holding the screen door open for Nash to enter behind her. The shady porch was filled with potted plants and wicker furniture. A good spot to have coffee and watch the sunrise, Eve thought. But despite the pleasant decor, there was something ominous about that space. She felt an inexplicable chill as she glanced through the screen out across the front yard.

"What is it?" Nash asked.

"Nothing. Just being cautious."

Turning, she moved up to the front door and rapped on the glass. When no one answered, Nash called out. "Mr. Naples, this is Chief Nash Bowden with the Black Creek Police Department. Can you please open the door?"

Eve listened for a moment. "I hear voices. Sounds like the TV."

Nash peered through the glass. "No sign of life that I

can see. Go on around back, but keep your eyes peeled. Holler if you see anything."

Eve nodded and exited the porch. Already the adrenaline had started to pump, though she couldn't say why. Nothing seemed particularly out of place. The area was quiet and peaceful and yet she felt the same knotted tension in her stomach that she'd experienced yesterday at the lab. The same dreaded certainty that something dark had entered her life.

The foreboding deepened as she rounded the corner of the house. Sweat trickled down her back and dampened her T-shirt. She was glad for the weight of the Glock at her hip. She'd never had to draw her weapon in the line of duty, and she hoped today would be no exception. But someone had deliberately tried to run them down on the side of the highway. Nash's tire had been sabotaged and his house searched. What was going on here? Why had the anonymous caller warned him away from the bones?

Eve's mind raced as she moved into the backyard. The man she'd seen in the parking lot had been no older than midfifties so he couldn't have been Ron Naples. How was Naples connected to that mysterious man and to the anonymous woman on the phone? How were any of them connected to John Doe?

Pausing at the top of the back porch steps, Eve quickly surveyed her surroundings. A dozen or more flies clung to the porch screen, their greenish blue iridescence shimmering in the dappled sunlight. Overhead, a pair of buzzards circled. The still air smelled fusty, an earthy aroma of mud, moss and something Eve didn't want to name. Her heart thudded erratically, and she felt lightheaded as she turned in a slow circle, her gaze spanning the shade trees and the expanse of yard that sloped steeply down to the water's edge. A fishing boat bobbed at the end of the dock.

Something else bobbed just beneath the surface.

Eve froze in horror. Then, with a sharp intake of breath, she bolted down the steps and dashed across the yard.

NASH WADED INTO the shallow water to give Eve a hand as she tried to drag the body ashore. He'd heard her frantic yell all the way around the house to the front porch and his heart had pounded in dread as he raced toward the sound of her voice. She was still calling out to him when he half ran, half skidded down the slanted lawn. By the time he got to the bank, she'd already plunged into the river to grab the corpse.

"He's dead," she said over her shoulder when he called her name.

"I can see that." Nash grabbed the man's arms.

"I didn't know he was dead," she said in a rush. "When I first saw him beneath the water, I thought there was a slim chance he could still be alive. My only thought was to get him out of the water."

"You did the right thing." Nash kept his tone low and even. Her adrenaline was in overdrive. "Just relax. I've got him." He pulled the man out of the water and went through the routine of checking for a heartbeat and pulse even though it was obvious he had been dead for at least several hours, if not a day or more.

The deceased looked to be in his late seventies, fully dressed in khaki Bermuda shorts, a cotton button-up shirt and boat shoes. No sign of a violent attack that Nash could see, but he wouldn't touch the body again until someone from the medical examiner's office arrived. The ME or his investigator would take control of the corpse, running a series of preliminary tests at the scene and then overseeing transport to the morgue.

Rising, Nash cast a glance around their surroundings as he made the necessary calls. The day seemed unnaturally quiet except for the buzz of the blowflies and the soft click of Eve's camera phone.

"We'll need to set a perimeter while we wait," he told her. "There's tape in the SUV. You know the drill. Seal all the doors and the side gate. No one but authorized personnel gets through."

"Are we looking at Ron Naples?" Eve asked as she lingered for a moment longer, her gaze riveted on the dead man.

"Given the description and location, I think that's a pretty safe bet. We'll get verification soon enough. The most important thing right now is to protect the body and preserve the scene."

Eve still couldn't seem to tear her gaze from the corpse. "What's going on, Nash? Ron Naples's car nearly runs us down on the highway last night and now we find him lying facedown in the river. That can't be a coincidence." She glanced up, her blue eyes shadowed. "Everything that's happened seems to be connected to the discovery of John Doe's remains, but how?"

"We don't know anything at this point. Could be

nothing more than an accidental drowning." Although an accident seemed doubtful. Like Eve, Nash didn't believe a coincidence likely, but it was best not to draw conclusions until the body had been properly examined and autopsied.

He moved back from the bank, where more blowflies had vectored in on the corpse. Left undisturbed, they'd lay their eggs in all the bodily orifices and first-stage maggots would appear within twenty-four hours. Nash appreciated the value of forensic entomology as much as the next law enforcement officer, but the carrion feeders always gave him the creeps.

Eve, on the other hand, seemed mostly undisturbed by the insect activity. She didn't shy away from the body or the blowflies, merely waved one away from her face as she continued to study the deceased.

"You really think this was an accident?" she asked.

"I think it's possible." Nash rubbed the back of his neck vigorously, where the flesh had started to crawl. "No visible wounds on the body. No sign of a struggle in the immediate vicinity."

Eve wasn't buying it. "It would certainly be a convenient accident if Ron Naples knew who murdered our John Doe."

Nash tried to rein her in. Tunnel vision was the enemy of every good investigator. "Let's not get too far ahead of ourselves. At this point, it's all guesswork."

She nodded and rose. "I'll set the perimeter."

"After you're finished, wait out front and try to keep the gawkers at bay until we can get some uniforms out here."

She nodded again and took off. He watched until she'd disappeared around the corner of the house and then he turned back to the water and the corpse. What *was* going on here? And why did he have the nagging suspicion that Eve was keeping something from him? She'd been acting strange ever since they'd left the lab yesterday afternoon.

He told himself he was overreacting to her reticence. He tried to put his doubts aside and concentrate on the more immediate mission of protecting the scene, but every few minutes his mind would wander back to the lab, back to the expression on her face when Allison Forester had held up the Mercury dime.

She knows something.

Let's not get ahead of ourselves.

The first squad car arrived in less than ten minutes, followed by the department's crime-scene tech and finally the medical examiner, a heavyset man dressed in an ill-fitting suit. His name was Dan Wexler. Nash had worked with Dr. Wexler for years and found him to be both cooperative and intuitive. Despite his rumpled appearance and lackadaisical demeanor, he could be a real bulldog when all the pieces of a puzzle didn't fit neatly together, a trait Nash greatly appreciated.

By the time Dr. Wexler scrambled down the slope to the bank, he was sweating profusely. He shrugged out of his suit coat, then hung it from a nearby tree branch and mopped his face with a white handkerchief.

"What have we got?" he asked Nash as he wheezed into the handkerchief.

"Looks like a drowning. No sign of a struggle in the

immediate vicinity. No visible marks on the body except for a few superficial scrapes on his face."

Wexler eyed him sagely. "I sense reservation. You have reason to suspect foul play?"

"Nothing concrete, but we need to keep an open mind on this one." Nash glanced over his shoulder. "House belongs to one Ron Naples, seventy-eight-year-old white male."

"Description matches the victim." Wexler set his case on the ground and wiped his face. His complexion had turned an alarming mottled red in the heat. From the man's coloring and labored breathing, Nash was a little concerned he might soon have two corpses on his hands.

"You okay?"

"You mean other than being old, overweight and out of shape?" Wexler stuffed the handkerchief in his pocket. "Yeah, I'm good. You check for identification?"

"No. Except for pulling him from the water, he hasn't been touched."

"We'll run his prints regardless of what we find in his pockets. Neighbors could probably help out with next of kin, but I don't imagine you want any of them traipsing down here just yet."

"We're trying to keep everything buttoned up until CSU has a chance to walk the scene," Nash said.

Wexler glanced out over the river as he rolled up his sleeves. "Feel that? There's a slight breeze coming off the water. That always helps with the smell. Better to find them outside than inside, I always say. Nothing like that stench trapped inside four walls in the middle of summer to turn a strong stomach, and I reckon mine is about as strong as they come." He knelt with some difficulty beside the deceased, opened his case and got down to business. Nash watched from a distance as the ME began his preliminary tests and examination.

"No maggots yet that I can see." He waved aside a fly. "Was the body submerged or floating?"

"Submerged, although he'd already been moved by the time I arrived on the scene. Detective Jareau found the body. She went in after him because she thought he might still be alive."

"I'll need to speak with her. Position of the body can give us an idea of how long he's been in the water. When gases build up and release, a body tends to float to the top."

"So taking that into consideration, what do you think?"

"It's still too early to say with any certainty, but given the position and condition of the body, I'd estimate less than twenty-four hours. If you were to twist my arm, I'd say eight to ten hours. Don't take any of that to the bank. Time of death is hard to pinpoint under these circumstances because the body temperature and rate of decomposition are skewed by the water." Wexler moved around to the other side of the body. "I see some predation around the eyes, so the scavengers had time to find him. Those cutaneous abrasions on his face are probably from scraping against the sandy river bottom." He checked the dead man's hands for wrinkling and *cutis anserine*—goose bumps.

"Anything strike you as out of the ordinary?" Nash asked.

"Hard to say until we get him undressed, washed and on the table."

Now that the uniforms were stationed out front, Eve had returned to await Wexler's preliminary analysis. Nash tracked her from his periphery as she walked to the end of the dock and peered into a small fishing boat. Then she conferred briefly with one of the crime-scene techs. The young officer came over and plucked something from the bottom of the boat, bagging and tagging the item to add to the growing pile.

After a few moments, Eve left the dock and joined Nash on the bank.

He stood. "What did you find?"

She shaded her eyes and nodded toward the end of the dock. "I spotted an empty whiskey bottle rolling around in the boat, which means you could be right about a drowning accident. I still find the timing suspect, but it's possible Mr. Naples had too much to drink and fell in the water. That could also explain his erratic driving, but only if you ignore the anonymous call you received afterward." She looked as if she wanted to comment further on the caller, but instead changed the subject as she inspected the corpse with a frown. "Does he look familiar to you?"

Nash studied her expression. "No, why? Have you seen him before?"

"I don't think so."

"But?" he pressed.

She shrugged. "I keep trying to put him in that car

last night. I'm certain he's not the man I saw in the parking lot. He's too old. As to the car on the highway… I'm hoping something else will come back to me."

"I was there, too," Nash said. "The glare of headlights on rain was blinding."

"I know, but that car came so close to me. I should have seen something."

"That car came way too close," he reminded her. "There wasn't time to think about anything except getting out of the way."

Dr. Wexler rose and motioned to Nash. He joined the man at the water's edge.

"What can you tell us?" Nash asked.

"It's still mostly guesswork, but I don't see anything that challenges my original assessment. The body was likely in the water for at least eight to ten hours."

"That would put time of death around midnight last night," Nash said. Well after he'd received the anonymous phone call.

"As to cause of death, I won't know for certain until I check his lungs. Even then, a drowning diagnosis is more about circumstances than tests, most of which are unreliable," Wexler explained. "If there are no obvious external injuries, we'll look at the organs and the victim's medical records to determine a natural cause—heart attack, stroke, a seizure of some kind. Any event that could have precipitated the deceased's fall into the water. The lab will run a full toxicology screen to check for drugs and blood alcohol content."

"How soon can we expect the autopsy?" Nash asked.

"We'll need to do it as quickly as possible. Now that

he's out of the water, decomposition will accelerate." Wexler removed his gloves and wiped his hands on the white handkerchief. "Meanwhile, I'm done here. We'll bag him up and get him to the morgue. I'll let you know as soon as he's on the schedule."

"You said you wanted to speak to the detective who found him," Nash reminded him.

Wexler glanced up the bank to where Eve stood. "That her?"

"Yes. Detective Eve Jareau."

"Pretty girl, but don't tell her I said so. I don't mean any disrespect. It's just in my line of work, you tend to observe and enjoy beauty whenever and wherever you can."

Nash rolled his eyes. "She's a good investigator. That's all you need to observe."

"Didn't mean to offend." Wexler tucked the handkerchief back in his pocket. "I'll need some of your boys to lend a hand with the body."

Nash motioned to a couple of the uniformed officers and told them what was needed. Two of them went to fetch the gurney from Wexler's vehicle while another two helped bag the body.

Eve moved up beside him, her gaze scanning the scenery. "This place is neat as a pin. Grass freshly cut, trees and bushes meticulously trimmed."

"Not what you'd expect from a heavy drinker," Nash said.

"My thoughts exactly. Maybe that whiskey bottle was planted in the boat to make us think his death was an accident. Maybe Ron Naples wasn't the one driving his car last evening when we were almost run down."

"That's a lot of maybes, Detective."

"Do you disagree?"

"Let's wait and see what the autopsy turns up. Go check inside the house and see what you can find. I'll take the garage."

"The garage is empty," Eve informed him. "I already looked for a dark sedan."

That gave Nash pause. "Maybe he left his car somewhere last night. Maybe he panicked and ditched it after he sideswiped us."

"That's a whole lot of maybes, Chief. I'm thinking it was stolen. That would explain a lot."

Nash had been thinking the same thing. "We need to find that car."

She nodded, but still didn't move away from the bank.

"What is it?" he asked.

She hesitated. "I know you said we shouldn't get ahead of ourselves, but what does your gut tell you about everything that's happened in the past twenty-four hours?"

"That's a tricky question. Yesterday, I would have considered a drowning accident a strong possibility. No reason to believe otherwise. Today…" His gaze drifted back to the bank. "Let's just say, we need to process the scene as if we already know what happened. We'll only get one shot at recovering uncontaminated evidence."

"Yes, sir."

He frowned at her formality.

Oblivious to his disapproval, she lifted a hand to shade her eyes as she scanned the opposite bank where a few rooftops peeked out of the trees. "By midnight last night the rain had stopped and the moon was up. Anyone sitting out on one of those docks might have seen something."

"Once we finish here, we'll start canvassing," he said. "Find out if there's a Mrs. Naples in the picture or anyone else living here. And look for a photo of Mr. Naples inside."

She nodded and without another word walked away. Nash watched her climb the porch steps and pause at the top to twist her hair into a bun at her nape. Then, pulling on a pair of latex gloves, she disappeared inside the house.

He turned back to the river. Now that the body had been moved, the area once again seemed peaceful. The breeze was cool and refreshing, the lapping water against the dock almost hypnotic. But something dark lingered. Not a scent or any piece of evidence, but a feeling deep in his gut that the final shoe had yet to drop.

Lifting his gaze, he scanned the trees, where the ruffling leaves sounded like whispers. What were they trying to tell him? What secrets did this place hold?

Sunlight danced on the surface of the water, drawing his gaze once more to the river. He tried to picture the scene. Had Ron Naples come down to the dock after the rain last night? Facing the water, he might not have noticed a silhouette creeping down from the bank until it was too late. But why ambush a seventy-eight-year-old retiree? Merely to steal his car? Or had Ron Naples known something that got him killed?

Nash knew he should take his own advice and wait for the autopsy, but he had a very bad feeling about Naples's death. A seventy-eight-year-old man sideswipes a police vehicle, almost taking out the detective working a cold case, and less than twenty-four hours later, he turns up dead from an apparent drowning accident.

Was Eve right? Had someone else been driving that dark sedan last night?

And what did any of this have to do with the skeletal remains recovered in a cave at the edge of town, much less with his ex-wife's kidnapping of a four-year-old child?

Too many loose ends. Too many seemingly random events in a short amount of time. So much for living in a sleepy small town.

He turned as one of his forensics techs came down the bank toward him. He was young and ambitious and would likely be snapped up by a larger department with a bigger budget just when Nash was coming to rely on his proficiency. "Find anything?"

"The usual assortment of prints and fibers inside the house. No sign of a break-in or struggle. I'll take what we've collected up to Tallahassee and see what the lab can piece together for us. Anything in particular I should tell them to look for?"

"Anything out of the ordinary. Anything that sets off alarm bells."

"That doesn't exactly set parameters, Chief."

Nash gave the man a curt nod. "Just keep looking and let me know what you find."

The tech went about his business while Nash headed around the house to the detached garage. He peered through a window into the empty bay and then tried the side door. It opened with a squeak. He entered cautiously and felt along the wall for a light switch.

The garage, like the rest of the property, was neat and orderly with shelving along one wall to hold an assortment of paint cans, hand tools and jars of nails and screws. Lawn equipment was tucked neatly underneath the shelves, leaving enough floor space for one midsize sedan.

Nash walked around the area slowly, letting his gaze linger here and there before landing on a corkboard mounted above a worktable. Several notes and to-do lists had been pinned to the board, along with a photograph of a gray-haired man and a young woman. Nash detected a resemblance. The man was Ron Naples, and he assumed the female was a close relative, possibly a daughter. He removed the pin and pocketed the photograph.

Then he backtracked to the center of the garage, where a dark stain marred the concrete floor. He knelt and ran his finger along the edge of the spot. An oil leak. Seemed odd that a man who maintained his property so meticulously would neglect a potentially costly problem with his vehicle. The oil seemed relatively fresh. Maybe Mr. Naples hadn't yet noticed.

Nash finished inspecting the garage and then went back around to the front of the house, where a few neighbors and onlookers had gathered at the edge of the road. Some had walked over from their homes while others had left their vehicles along the curb. They had congregated in a tight little group, their gazes riveted on Nash as they spoke in low tones to one another. He went over to them. A few shuffled their feet and looked uncomfortable, not sure what to say or how to feel in the face of someone else's tragedy.

A man stepped forward, separating himself from the others. "What's going on?" he demanded. "We saw all the police cars parked out front. Did something happen to Ron?"

"How well did you know Mr. Naples?" Nash asked.

The man looked alarmed. "How well *did* I know him? Are you saying he's dead?"

"Of course he's dead," someone behind him piped up. "We saw them load up the body."

The first speaker turned back to Nash. "What happened? We're all Ron's friends and neighbors. I've lived across the road from the man for nearly fifteen years. Seems to me we have a right to know."

"Were you close?" Nash asked.

The man considered the question. "I guess I'm as close a friend as he has around here. Ron's a bit of a loner. Not easy to get to know until he's been around you for a while. He moved down here from Tallahassee when he retired. Wanted a quieter life, he said. His daughter still lives in the city. He drives over to visit her every other week or so. Drove." He corrected himself with a grimace. "Damn."

"Let's speak in private," Nash suggested. The man

looked around at the group, then shrugged and followed Nash away from the curious onlookers.

"What's your name?" Nash asked.

"Walt Pearlman. Like I said, I live just across the road."

Nash gave the man a quick assessment. Pearlman looked to be in his late sixties, tall and trim with silver hair and a thick salt-and-pepper mustache. He was dressed like most of his neighbors in cargo shorts, a T-shirt and flip-flops.

"When was the last time you saw Mr. Naples?"

His brow furrowed as he thought back. "A couple of days ago, if memory serves. We both walked out to check our mailboxes at the same time."

"Did you notice anything unusual about his demeanor?"

"Not that I recall. We only spoke for a moment or two. He collected his mail and went back into the house."

"Did he seem distracted or upset?"

"No, but like I said, Ron was a loner. He didn't always stop to shoot the breeze like the rest of us do."

"Can you see Mr. Naples's property from your house?"

"Only if I'm sitting on the front porch or looking out the kitchen window. Look here, Detective—"

"Chief Nash Bowden."

He acknowledged the correction with a brief nod. "What happened to Ron? Heart attack?"

"Why do you think it was a heart attack? Did he have any health problems that you know of?"

"No. As a matter of fact, he seemed healthy as a horse, but the man was pushing eighty. Things start to go south for all of us after a certain age no matter how well we take care of ourselves." He paused. "So what happened to him, Chief Bowden?"

"I'm not at liberty to divulge the details of his death until we've notified next of kin."

The man's expression sobered as he nodded his understanding. "That would be his daughter, Lacy. She's his only family. Ron and his wife split up years ago."

"Is this her?" Nash took out the photograph he'd found in the garage.

"Yeah, although that picture must have been taken a few years back."

"You said Mr. Naples drove to Tallahassee regularly to see her. Do you know if he made that trip yesterday?"

"I doubt it unless she had some sort of emergency. He was there just last weekend."

"Would you happen to have her name and phone number?"

"I can get it for you, no problem. Ron gave me her contact information in case anything ever happened to him. You reach a certain age and you start to think about things like that. About dying alone and no one finding your body until days or weeks later."

"Did you see Mr. Naples's vehicle leave or return late yesterday afternoon?"

"No, but if I had the TV on, I probably wouldn't have heard his car."

"What about during the night?"

"Ron wouldn't have gone out at night, regardless. His eyesight was starting to fail him."

"Was he known to drink alone?"

"Ron? Never saw him drink anything stronger than black coffee." Pearlman shook his head. "Poor Lacy. Ron always spoke about her with so much pride. They were really close. His death will hit her hard."

Nash gently steered him back. "Did you notice if he had any visitors during the past few days? Any strange cars in the neighborhood? Anything at all out of the ordinary that you can think of?"

Walt Pearlman was silent for a moment as he digested that particular line of questioning. "You're not saying… What are you saying, Chief? That Ron was *murdered*?"

"These are just routine questions," Nash explained. "Please don't jump to any conclusions."

"It's hard not to when you won't say what happened to him."

"We're waiting for the autopsy," Nash said. "Until then I'd appreciate your discretion. I'd hate for anything to get back to Mr. Naples's daughter before I have a chance to speak with her."

Pearlman nodded. "Yeah, sure. I won't say anything, but people are going to talk. It's human nature, especially in a place like this. Lots of retirees out here on the river. Lots of people with time on their hands."

Nash glanced back at the group of neighbors. They were all watching avidly from a distance.

"If you wouldn't mind getting me the daughter's contact information, I'd appreciate it," he said.

Walt Pearlman started back toward the crowd, then turned suddenly and came back over to Nash. "You asked about visitors. This is probably not what you had in mind, but there was a car with a cleaning company logo parked in Ron's driveway day before yesterday. That would have been Wednesday."

"Cleaning company? You mean like a biweekly housecleaning service?"

"His regular cleaning lady retired a few months back and moved to Orlando to be with her family. I didn't think much of it when I saw the car in his driveway. I figured Ron had hired the service to take Maria's place. He was a bit of a neat freak. He liked things done a certain way, but he was getting too old to do everything himself."

"Do you remember the name of the cleaning service?" Nash asked.

"It's the one with the crown on the mop. You see their vehicles all over town."

"King's Maid Services."

"That's the one."

The same company Nash used. Another coincidence?

He was beginning to think nothing that had happened since John Doe's remains had been removed from that cave was by chance.

"Thank you for your cooperation, Mr. Pearlman."

"I'm glad I could help. I'll just head over to my place and get Lacy's number for you. If you need anything else, let me know."

Nash turned back to the house, where Eve stood staring at him from the front steps. He crossed the yard to join her.

"Anything?"

She shook her head. "The inside is as neat as the outside. Everything cleaned, dusted and freshly vacuumed. I don't know if that means anything."

"The neighbor noticed a vehicle here on Wednesday from a cleaning company. King's Maid Services. It's the same outfit I've been using for the past few months."

She lifted a brow. "Do they have a key to your house?"

"Yes."

"We can assume they also had a key to Mr. Naples's house. What do you make of that?"

"It's a long shot, but it could explain how someone was able to enter my place without breaking in," Nash said. "We should find out if the same person cleaned both homes. That could be our common denominator."

Eve nodded. "I'm on it."

"I know where their office and warehouse are located downtown. We can stop by on our way back to the station."

She hesitated with a slight frown then acquiesced. "Sounds good. I have a couple of other leads I want to chase down this afternoon."

Nash was immediately on alert. "Anything you care to share?"

"Let me see if anything pans out first. I'll keep you posted."

What the hell are you keeping from me? Nash wondered again as she came down the steps and brushed past him.

Maybe she was just being territorial. That would explain her reluctance to share leads. But Eve had never struck him as the type to allow ego to interfere in an investigation. He searched for another benign reason for her reticence. She liked to work alone, so maybe she felt awkward or even resentful of his intrusion into the case. On reflection, neither excuse held much water for Nash. Eve was a professional.

Whatever she was keeping from him regarding the John Doe case, Nash would uncover her secrets one way or another.

Chapter Six

King's Maid Services was located in a nondescript industrial park on the outskirts of downtown Black Creek. Loaded semitrucks lumbered down the narrow streets, slowing normal traffic to a crawl. Nash finally maneuvered around one of the vehicles, only to be stopped by flashing lights and descending crossbars at the railroad tracks bisecting the park. He drummed his fingers impatiently on the steering wheel while Eve stared out the side window.

"Bad timing," he muttered.

She turned with a frown. "What do you mean?"

He nodded toward the tracks. "I'm talking about the train. What did you think I meant?"

"Nothing. I was lost in thought, I guess." She looked momentarily disconcerted. "I keep thinking about Ron Naples and wondering if he knew something about the John Doe case that got him killed."

"*If* he was murdered," Nash stressed. "Hopefully the autopsy will provide a few clues if not a definitive cause of death."

"Yes, let's hope." She turned back to the window and

fell silent. Nash didn't try to pursue further conversation, but instead used the opportunity to check his messages and then fiddle with the rearview mirror and the AC while they waited for the train to pass. It wasn't like him to be so restless. There was a time when he could spend hours on a stakeout without getting antsy, but the quieter and more introspective Eve became, the more impatient he found himself. Maybe it was for the best they go their separate ways that afternoon. He needed to do some hard thinking on this case. Needed to sit in a quiet place and try to connect some dots.

Finally the crossing bar lifted and he drove across the tracks, checking addresses before he turned down one of the rows of warehouses. He located the crown-and-mop logo painted on the plateglass window and pulled into a spot in the common parking area. A few people were coming and going from the stone-countertop company at the end, but the spaces on either side of King's Maid Services looked to be empty, attesting to the hard times that had fallen on area businesses.

Eve opened the door and paused on the threshold to survey the interior. Then she held the door open for Nash. He took off his sunglasses and stuck them in his shirt pocket as he glanced around the sparsely furnished office. A few minutes ticked by before a woman wearing jeans and a T-shirt with the same logo came in from the back. She looked to be around forty, a petite brunette with hazel eyes that opened wide in shock when she took in their guns and badges.

"What's happened?" Her hand flew to her heart. "Is it my son—"

"We're here about one of your clients," Nash quickly explained.

She closed her eyes on a relieved breath. "Thank goodness. My boy is stationed overseas. He's been away for nearly a year, but I still have a tendency to fear the worst."

Nash gave her a sympathetic nod. "We didn't mean to alarm you. I'm Nash Bowden with the Black Creek Police Department and this is Detective Eve Jareau."

She glanced from one to the other as she sat down on the edge of the desk. "How can I help you? You say you're here about one of our clients?"

"Are you the owner of the business?" Eve asked.

"Yes, sorry. I'm still a bit rattled. It's not every day the police come walking through my door. Anyway, I'm Delia Middleton. My maiden name was King." She tapped the logo on her shirt. "I took over the business after my dad died last year."

"We're here about Ron Naples," Eve told her. "His house is on River Road near Myrtle Cove. One of your vehicles was seen in his driveway day before yesterday. We'd like you to check your records and tell us who you sent out there to clean his house that day."

Delia Middleton looked uneasy. "May I ask why you need that information? Has he filed a claim against one of my employees?"

Eve pounced. "Were you expecting him to?"

"No, of course not. It's just… I can't think of any other reason the police would be here asking me to pull my records."

"Mr. Naples is dead," Nash said. "We're trying to

piece together what happened. Talking to the people who last saw him alive is routine."

"He's dead?" She looked shocked. "What happened to him?"

"As I said, we're still trying to piece it together. Can you tell us who cleaned his house the day before yesterday?"

She rose. "Yes, of course. It'll take me a minute to pull up his file. I think I already know but let me make certain." She went around the desk and sat down at the computer. "Normally, we work in teams of two," she explained. "That makes moving furniture easier. Except for office buildings, of course. Depending on the size, we may send as many as four if we can spare the personnel."

"We're only interested in Mr. Naples." While he conversed with Delia Middleton, Eve had positioned herself at the window so that she could peek at the computer screen.

"I'm getting to Mr. Naples," Delia said. "He was an exception to our two-member crew. He was very uncomfortable around strangers. He would allow only one person in his home at a time. Despite that restriction, he was particular about how he wanted things done. His usual house cleaner has been with us for years. Mary is very good with people and she and Mr. Naples got on well. She's been servicing his home for the past month and he seemed satisfied with her performance. But she called in sick this week and we had to send someone else out to his house."

"Who took her place?" Nash asked.

The woman glanced up with a frown. "One of our new employees. Nadine Crosby."

"How new?"

"She started on Monday. Walked in cold asking for a job. I don't normally hire without a trial run, but we were shorthanded and Nadine had references and could start immediately."

"If Mr. Naples was as picky as you say, wasn't it risky sending someone unproven out to his house alone?" Nash asked.

"I explained about Mary's illness and asked if he'd like to reschedule, but he insisted we keep to our regular routine. I had no one else available in his time slot so I decided to take a chance on Nadine."

"Can you tell us where we can find her?"

Delia bit her lip. "I wish I could. I'm afraid she didn't come to work today."

"Did she call in sick?"

"No. She just didn't show up."

"Did you try calling her?"

"No answer." Delia turned from the computer screen and folded her hands on the desk as she glanced up at Nash. "Do you know that feeling you get when your instincts warn you not to do something, but you go against your better judgment and do it anyway? I knew Nadine would be a headache from the moment she walked through the door. I could just tell. I'm not one to judge on appearances, but she had a look about her."

"What do you mean by that?" Nash asked.

She took a moment to answer. "You've heard the old saying, 'rode hard and put away wet?' That's Nadine

Crosby. I know that sounds harsh, but it's an apt description. Every mistake that poor woman ever made seems carved on her face. Plus, she's a smoker, and that can also take a toll. Not that she ever lit up around me," she hastily added. "We have a strict nonsmoking policy on the job, but I could smell it on her clothes every morning when she clocked in."

Nash thought about the raspy voice on the phone. *You need to leave them bones alone.*

"Is Nadine from around here?" Eve asked.

Delia rotated her chair to stare up at her. "Born and raised in Black Creek, but from what I understand, she left town years ago. She's only recently moved back."

"Did she say why she came back?"

"Her brother still lives here. I guess she wanted to be close to her remaining family."

"Have you ever met him?"

"The brother? Once when he came to pick up Nadine." Delia suppressed a shudder. "Talk about bad news."

"Why do you say that?"

"He had this look about him. It's hard to explain, but the way his gaze kept darting around the warehouse made me think he was scoping out anything valuable enough to steal. Put it this way. I would never want to meet him alone in a dark alley."

"Can you describe him?" Eve asked.

"Midfifties, maybe. Five nine—five ten, stocky build. Brown hair going gray. Dark eyes, same as Nadine. Piercing. Like he could see right through you."

"That's very precise," Eve said.

Delia grimaced. "He made an impression."

"Do you know his name?"

"Nadine called him Denton. I don't know if that's his first or last name. I guess it would be odd if she called her own brother by his last name, though."

Eve's line of questioning intrigued Nash. Was she trying to place the brother in Ron Naples's stolen sedan? Was he the mysterious man she'd seen in the lab parking lot?

Eve flashed him a glance as if she'd somehow sensed his curiosity. Her gaze said, *Trust me. I know what I'm doing.* He gave her a vague nod.

She turned her attention back to Delia with an answering nod. "Is Nadine younger or older than the brother?"

"A little younger, I'm guessing. She put down her age as fifty on her employment application."

"Do you have a photograph of her?"

"No, it's not a requirement for our records."

"Can you describe her?"

Delia paused. "Scrawny but tough. Rough around the edges, but a real hard worker when she bothers to show up."

"I'd like to take a look at her employment application," Eve said. Her tone remained polite, but she didn't make it sound like a request.

Delia balked, glancing from Eve to Nash as if hoping he would intervene. "I'm trying to be as cooperative as I can, but our employee records are confidential."

"We can get a warrant," Eve said. "But it'll be easier on all of us if we don't have to go that route."

Something flickered in the woman's eyes, a combination of anger, defiance and panic. Nash exchanged another glance with Eve. She knew as well as he they didn't have grounds for a warrant, not even close, but her hollow threat worked on Delia. She printed off a copy of the application and handed it to Eve without a word. She perused the single page with a furrowed brow and then passed the form to Nash.

He skimmed the information and glanced up. "This is her current address?"

"It's the only one I have on file." Delia's phone rang just then. She took it out of her pocket and glanced at the screen. "I'm sorry. I have to take this. It's one of our suppliers. I'll only be a moment." She got up and walked into the back room.

Eve had turned back to the window. "What do you think?" Nash asked as he rounded the desk and glanced at the computer screen.

"She seems a little cagey but that may just be nerves. Some people get jittery around the police."

Nash moved up beside her at the window. "Why all those questions about Nadine Crosby's brother? Do you know something I don't?"

Eve frowned. "No, of course not. It just seemed a viable angle after Delia mentioned him." She paused. "Doesn't it strike you as curious, or even opportune, that Nadine Crosby had only been on the job since Monday? She was sent alone to Ron Naples's house on Wednesday and two days later he's found dead, his car is missing and Nadine doesn't show up for work this morning."

Nash leaned a shoulder against the window frame as

he studied her expression. "You'd tell me if you learned something I needed to know about this case, right?"

"Like what?" She met his gaze without flinching, but there was a defensive quality to her voice and demeanor that made him wonder again about what she might be hiding.

"You've been acting strange ever since we left the lab yesterday." He tried not to sound accusing, but it came out that way despite his best effort.

She picked up on his tone and gave him a cool look. "Define strange."

"Quiet. Secretive."

"A lot has happened since we left the lab yesterday. What may seem secretive to you is contemplative to me. I told you. I can't stop thinking about this case."

"You said earlier you have a couple of leads you want to pursue on your own. Why?"

"It's nothing concrete—just a hunch. I don't want to waste your time if it doesn't pan out." She folded her arms. "Is this going to be a problem for you? You gave me a case that no one else wanted and told me I could run with it. Either I'm lead detective or I'm not. Either you trust me or you don't."

He was pushing things too far, Nash realized. His experiences with his ex-wife had made him too suspicious. Eve didn't deserve that. She was a good detective, perfectly capable of running her case as she saw fit and chasing down leads without his interference.

"You're right. I apologize. This case has gotten under my skin, too. It's been a stressful twenty-four hours."

She seemed to want to press the issue further, but

then thought better of it. "I'll go check around back and see if I can sniff out anything. It's stuffy in here anyway. I could use the fresh air."

"Wait a minute." He stopped her as she moved by him toward the door. "Are we good?"

She took a moment, then nodded. "Yeah, we're good."

"Eve…"

He wasn't sure what he meant to say to her. Maybe he just wanted to utter her name so that he had an excuse to study her upturned face, to let his gaze linger over the curve of her lips and the tiny errant strand of auburn hair that brushed against her cheek. He resisted the urge to tuck it back. Now was not the time or place. He doubted there would ever be a time and place for them. That ship had sailed years ago when he'd allowed Grace to dictate the terms of his freedom. Before that even, when he'd returned from Afghanistan with a bullet wound in his shoulder and a slew of nightmares that only grew more disturbing with the passage of time.

She cocked her head slightly. "Is there something else?"

He wondered if she'd noticed his hesitation. Wondered if she sensed the darkness that lay deep inside him. A darkness that his ex-wife had fed on, gathered strength from, but Eve was different. She could either be his salvation or his ruin and Nash wasn't about to take that gamble. "Just be careful."

His caution seemed to take her aback. Or was it something she'd read in his eyes? "Of course. I always am."

"I'm serious," he said. "It seems we kicked a hornet's

nest when we recovered those bones in that cave. You may not have secrets, but John Doe sure does."

He could have sworn he saw a shiver go through her. "Do you ever wonder if some secrets are best left buried?"

"That's an odd sentiment for a police detective."

A shadow darkened her expression as she wound a finger around the silver chain at her throat. Her eyes seemed liquid and fathomless. *An enigma wrapped in a riddle.* They'd worked together for the past six years and had shared the intimacy of a kiss, but at that moment, Nash had the feeling he didn't really know Eve Jareau at all.

She seemed to shake herself then and gave a nervous little laugh. "Maybe I'm more exhausted than I realized. I didn't sleep well last night."

"That makes two of us. Go around back and check things out," he said. "I'll finish in here."

After she left, he remained at the window, staring out. The sun beat down relentlessly on the parking lot. He scoured the line of vehicles, looking for a black sedan or the pickup truck he'd spotted the night before racing away from his house. For a moment, he considered the possibility that Delia Middleton could be his anonymous caller, but she didn't have the rasp or the deep country accent of the woman on the phone. Nadine Crosby seemed a more likely candidate.

Delia returned a moment later and said briskly, "You got what you came for. I've given you everything I have on Nadine Crosby. Good luck tracking her down."

He handed her a card. "Call me at this number if she gets in touch."

Delia wiped her hands nervously on the sides of her jeans. "Could I ask you a question before you leave?"

Nash nodded. "Go ahead."

"You think Nadine had something to do with Mr. Naples's death, don't you? She and her brother? That's why you're here asking all these questions about them."

"Neither is considered a suspect at the moment. As I mentioned earlier, we're looking to speak with anyone who may have last seen Mr. Naples alive." Nash walked to the door and then paused to glance back. "By the way, can you tell me who cleaned my house this week?"

The question seemed to take her by surprise. "Your house?"

"Your company sends a team to my place every Thursday," he said. "When I got home last night, someone had left an outside door open to my office."

She grew wary and defensive. "Are you blaming my people?"

"Not necessarily, but it would be helpful to know who was in my house yesterday."

She went back around to the computer and sat down, but she didn't tap any keys, merely stared straight ahead at the blank screen.

"Is something wrong?" Nash asked.

"I can't help wondering what my dad would have to say about all this." She seemed to be talking to herself. "He was such a good judge of character. Never in a million years would he have hired someone off the street the way I did. He was always so careful about vetting and references. You have to be when you're sending employees into private homes. The legal ramifications are enormous. I knew it was a mistake to hire her, but she caught me at a bad time. I was desperate for help, and to be honest, I felt sorry for her. It was obvious to me she'd had a rough life and I figured she needed the money. So I decided to give her a chance."

"Is that your way of telling me you sent Nadine Crosby to my house yesterday?"

Delia closed her eyes on a deep sigh. "Yes. She was a substitute for a member of your usual team." She cringed as if waiting for Nash to berate her.

"Where do you keep your clients' house keys?" he asked.

She blinked, as if the question had caught her off guard. "In a safe. I hand them out each morning as needed and the teams return them when they come in to clock out."

"Has anyone ever kept a key overnight?"

"Absolutely not. They'd be fired on the spot if they ever tried such a thing. I may be a pushover in certain areas, but I'm a stickler when it comes to my clients' house keys."

"Who has access to the safe?"

"Only me."

Nash slipped the folded employment application in his pocket. "Thanks for your help. We'll be in touch."

Outside, he put his sunglasses back on as he searched for Eve in the bright heat. He almost ran headlong into her coming around the building. He resisted the urge to put his hands on her shoulders to steady her. Or maybe to steady himself. Spending so much time with her was doing things to him. Making him think thoughts he had no right to.

"Sorry," she said. "I have a bad habit of rounding corners without looking."

"Did you find anything?"

"The back door was open. I took a peek inside. Nothing struck me as unusual. Just a bunch of cleaning equipment and supplies. How about you? Did you learn anything more about Nadine Crosby?"

"Only that she was a member of the team sent to clean my house yesterday."

Eve's eyes widened. "So we have that common denominator after all. But why would she leave the outside door of your office open when she could have easily glanced through the files on your desk while she was there?"

"Maybe she was afraid of getting caught. Or maybe someone else wanted a look at those files."

"Like her brother?"

Nash stared down into her upturned face, noting the vivid blue of her eyes and the way the sunlight caught the auburn highlights in her hair. He quickly glanced away. "Let's go find Nadine Crosby and ask her."

THE ADDRESS ON Nadine's employment application led them to a trailer park on the outskirts of Black Creek. The mobile homes were old, the paint faded and chipped, but the grounds were shady and pleasant. Nash located Nadine's place and pulled into the narrow driveway.

Ever since Delia Middleton had mentioned Nadine's

brother, Eve couldn't help wondering if they were the pair she'd glimpsed waiting for her father the night he left home. Had he unwittingly gotten into a car with his killers that night? Had he suspected what might happen when he came into her bedroom to say goodbye?

Eve's mind rolled back until she was once again at the window staring out into the darkness. She could see her father under the streetlight as he stored his belongings in the trunk and then climbed into the car beside the blonde without ever once turning to look back in regret. But the man in the back seat had glanced back. He'd met Eve's gaze and warned her to silence.

"The place looks deserted to me," Nash said. "You think she's already cut and run?"

"It's possible. Or maybe she just hasn't had a chance to settle in yet." But Nash was right. Like Ron Naples's house, the mobile home wore an air of abandonment. Save for Nash's vehicle, the driveway was empty, the blinds drawn at every window.

They climbed the wooden steps to the small porch and Nash knocked on the door. It opened silently and Eve peered around him to glance inside. She could make out the shapes of furniture in the dimly lit room, but little else. She sniffed the air. Nothing but the faint scent of marijuana drifting out from the shadows.

Nash pushed the door wider, letting in a shaft of sunlight. "Police! Anyone home?"

"Y'all looking for Nadine?"

Eve turned at the timid inquiry. An elderly woman with a walker observed them curiously from the back deck of the neighboring mobile home. She looked to be well into her seventies if not eighties, white-haired and stooped, but her gaze was razor sharp.

"Have you seen her today?" Eve asked.

"Not today, hon. She moved out. Packed everything up and took off in the middle of the night."

"When was this?"

"Last night around midnight or a little after."

Right around the time Ron Naples had drowned.

"I'm guessing she skipped out on her rent," the woman added. "They don't give you much leeway here. You fail to pay on time, they'll dump all your belongings on the curb."

"Did she say where she was going?" Eve asked.

"I didn't talk to her. The commotion she made loading up her truck woke me up. I looked out my bedroom window and saw her make three or four trips back and forth to her trailer. Then she drove off and hasn't been back since."

Eve walked to the edge of the porch and tried to assume a friendly demeanor. "Do you know if she has friends or family in the area that she might be staying with? Her brother, maybe?"

"I didn't even know she had a brother, but come to think of it, there's been a man coming around once or twice." A breeze ruffled the woman's cotton-fluff hair as she gazed off in the distance, her eyes narrowing as she thought back. "Husky fellow. About yay high." She measured the air several inches above her head. "None of my business who he was or why he was here, but I didn't like the looks of him. I could tell he was trouble from a mile away. Now that you mention a brother, though, he and Nadine did bicker like siblings. I could hear them through my window."

"What did they argue about?"

"I couldn't hear them that well. Just a word or two here and there. But in my experience, a guy like that almost always comes around when he needs money."

"Do you know his name?" Nash asked.

"Only thing I ever heard Nadine call him was bastard."

"Can you describe him?" Eve asked.

"Not tall, not short. Stout but not fat. Brownish hair, best I recall." She shrugged. "I never looked too close. I figured it best to keep my distance."

"What about Nadine? Can you describe her?"

"Skinny as a fence rail, that one. Meth head, most likely. You see that wasted look a lot around here." She glanced across the space between them. "Sometimes I'd see her sitting out there on the steps after dark drinking beer and smoking one cigarette after another. I tried to strike up a conversation a few times, but she made it clear she didn't want to be bothered by the neighbors."

"What about eye and hair color?" Eve asked.

"Her eyes reminded me of the muscadine grapes that grew wild in the woods where I grew up. Dark with almost a purplish hue. And intense. Like she was thinking bad thoughts when she looked at you. Her hair's white like mine, only from a bottle, I think." She shrugged. "That's about all I can tell you."

"Was she close with any of the other residents?" Nash asked.

"Like I said, she kept to herself. Never saw her so much as nod in anyone else's direction."

"You said she drives a truck?"

"An old pickup. Don't know the make or model, but it made a God-awful racket when she took off last night."

"What about the man she argued with? What kind of vehicle did he drive?"

"Couldn't tell you that. I never saw him drive up. He either walked here or left his car in the public parking area out front." She shifted her weight against the walker, her gaze darting from Nash to Eve and then back. "Now I got a question for the two of you. What did she do?"

"Nothing that we know of," Nash said.

"She must have done something or you wouldn't be here. Is she dead?"

Eve gave her a puzzled look. "Why would you ask that?"

"I've been around for a long time. In my experience, things don't end well for people like Nadine."

"She's very much alive as far as we know," Eve assured her.

"Well, then, somebody else must have died. Either way, Nadine Crosby is long gone from this place."

Chapter Seven

A search of the mobile home yielded little more than a trash can full of beer bottles and a pair of overflowing ashtrays. The cheap furniture had been left behind, but the beds had been stripped and the cupboards emptied. Whether she'd been involved in Ron Naples's death or not, Nadine Crosby obviously didn't plan on returning to the trailer.

Back at the station, Eve and Nash parted ways. He disappeared into his office while she climbed into her own vehicle and headed out. She parked down the street from her mother's house and reconnoitered for several minutes even though she told herself she was being paranoid. Despite her mother's accident the night before, she'd gone into work that morning and wouldn't be home until after five.

But Eve was more worried about running into Wayne Brody. She wanted to make sure he wasn't hanging around on the pretext of fixing leaky faucets or sticking doors or whatever. He had a full-time job so hopefully he'd be occupied until Eve was long gone.

The aging neighborhood languished in the midafternoon heat. Eve rolled down her window, letting the nostalgic sounds of lawn mowers and yard sprinklers lull her for a moment while her mind drifted back to her childhood.

Despite the lingering trauma from her father's abandonment, she'd been a happy kid, or at least a contented one after Wayne moved out. She and her mother had always been close. They'd done everything together—shopping, movies, trips to the water park in the summer. Eve had missed her dad—would always miss that twinkle in his eyes and the bedtime stories he'd concocted from his own experiences—but the tension in the house had faded with his leaving. Jackie had seemed more relaxed and easygoing. Or so it had seemed at first. So she had tried to pretend.

Looking back, Eve realized she'd always sensed something bubbling beneath the surface that she hadn't understood. Her mother's blue eyes had been shadowed with something indefinable even when she'd laughed at her child's silly jokes.

Then Wayne had come along and there'd been a different kind of tension in the house. He and Jackie never argued, never so much as disagreed on what to have for dinner, but neither had there been much laughter or open affection. They'd seemed more like amiable roommates than husband and wife. Eve hadn't been old enough to analyze their short-lived marriage, but in retrospect she could only describe it as passionless, though they had shared a bedroom and almost certainly a bed.

She didn't want to think about that. Even now as an

adult, the thought of any intimacy between her mother and Wayne Brody made her queasy.

Taking another look around the neighborhood, she closed the car window and got out. Senses on alert, she kept a sharp eye out for any unfamiliar vehicles in the neighborhood in case she'd been followed from the station. Was someone watching her at that very moment?

She cast a wary glance over her shoulder as she crossed the street and turned up her mother's driveway. Making sure she was hidden from any prying eyes on the street, she retrieved the spare key from over the door and let herself into the mudroom.

She'd grown up in that house, was as familiar or more so with the layout and furnishings as she was with her own home. But stepping through the doorway into the kitchen felt as if she'd entered a stranger's abode. She didn't understand her apprehension. She didn't understand why she was looking back now and questioning that shadow in her mother's eyes and the way Jackie would sometimes jump when Eve walked into the room, as if she'd been a million miles away.

She called out softly, "Mom, you home?"

No one answered. No sound at all in the house except for the sudden pounding of her heartbeat in her ears.

What was going on here? Why was she suddenly on edge in her childhood home? Why was she suddenly so uncomfortable with her memories?

"Mom?"

She walked through the kitchen and down the hallway to her old bedroom, pausing to peek inside before she continued into her mother's room. She stood on the threshold and glanced around. She'd always been fascinated by Jackie's space. Everything so pristine and orderly. Bed neatly made. Not so much as a speck of dust on the dresser or chest, no stray clothing dropped on the floor or tossed onto the overstuffed armchair by the window.

Eve had always thought the room pleasant, but it hit her suddenly that her mother's private space was almost antiseptic with the soft gray walls and monochromatic linens. The room said nothing about Jackie's personality or her past.

When Eve left for college, Jackie had stressed that this would always be her home. She never needed permission to come over. But using the spare key to let herself into the house was one thing; searching her mother's bedroom another situation entirely. Eve would hate it if someone came into her home and went through her things. Bottom line, though, she was a cop, so she tamped down her misgivings and crossed the room to her mother's closet.

Eve had long ago discovered the boxes of mementos her mother kept shoved in a corner. She'd gone through them once looking for photographs of her father. Now she dug down through the keepsakes to uncover the school yearbooks at the bottom. Arranging them chronologically, she sat cross-legged on the floor and pored through the pages, running her finger down the list of names until she found the person she was looking for among the sophomores—a girl named Nadine Crosby.

Eve expelled a sharp breath, as if she'd taken a hard punch in the gut. She hadn't seen the blonde's face that night, had never known her name until now. *Nadine Crosby.*

Her hair was long in the photograph, but the same white-blond from Eve's memory. Her gaze was slightly hooded, her smile edging from shy to coy. She was attractive, but more striking than beautiful with her dark eyes contrasting so vividly against her platinum tresses.

So you're her. My dad's other woman.

After all these years, the blonde behind the wheel had a name and a face.

Eve thumbed back a page and located her mother's smiling image. She and Nadine Crosby had gone to school together, had likely been in some of the same classes. How well had Jackie known her? Had her mother suspected the icy blonde was the reason her husband had left her? Or was she as oblivious to the other woman's identity as she claimed?

After the initial shock, Eve went back to the beginning of the yearbook and traced the names in her father's senior class until she stopped once more on the name Crosby. Denton Crosby. *I could tell he was trouble from a mile away.*

Yes, Eve thought. He'd had that look even in high school. Dark, intense eyes. A sneer instead of a smile. Tough guy. Bad news all around.

Eve had met guys like Denton Crosby both in her line of work and as a child when her father's friends had come around. Despite Gabriel Jareau's charm and easygoing demeanor, he'd been drawn to people like Nadine and Denton Crosby, people who flaunted laws and social mores. People her mother would never allow into the house when they showed up on their motorcycles or in their souped-up cars with loud mufflers.

In Eve's mind, she could see Denton Crosby looking out the car window, zeroing in on her bedroom window as if he'd somehow known she was watching them.

Of course, she could be wrong about the brother and sister. She had no real proof they were the pair who'd waited in the car for her father that night. She hadn't been able to see either of them clearly. There came a point, though, when a string of events could no longer be considered coincidental.

After returning everything to the box except for the one yearbook, she shoved her mother's keepsakes back into the corner of the closet. She moved into the bedroom and was just heading out into the hallway when a sound stopped her cold. Someone had come in through the back door.

She thought at first her mother had come home from work early. Eve tried to come up with an appropriate excuse for being in Jackie's house in the middle of the day. She waited for the familiar click of her mother's heels on the parquet floor, but nothing came to her except a tense, waiting silence.

Inching her way along the wall, she peered through the small dining room into the kitchen. A man stood at the open refrigerator taking stock of the contents. Then, grabbing a beer from the door, he turned and fumbled through the nearest drawer for an opener.

Wayne Brody tossed the lid in the garbage, then took a long swallow from the bottle as he moseyed from the kitchen through the dining room and into the den. He walked around the room, touching this, touching that, before pausing in front of the window to stare out at the street.

Eve didn't know what to make of his behavior, nor could she figure out why she didn't confront him. *Wayne, what the hell do you think you're doing?* His conduct seemed odd and overly familiar even for Wayne. So instead she hung back in the hallway, pressing her back against the wall as she watched him.

After a moment, he returned to the kitchen and polished off the beer while retrieving his toolbox from the mudroom. Disposing of the empty, he grabbed another bottle from the fridge and ambled back into the dining room, but this time he headed for the hallway instead of the den.

He was coming straight toward her. Still unsure of why she felt the need to hide from her mother's ex-husband, she scurried back to Jackie's bedroom and tracked Wayne through a crack in the door. She told herself he could have a perfectly innocent reason for his visit. Maybe he'd come back to finish the leaky faucet task he'd abandoned the evening before when Jackie cut her hand. Maybe Eve felt the need to conceal her presence because Wayne Brody wasn't the only one violating her mother's privacy.

He paused at the bathroom and bent to set the toolbox on the floor. Then he slowly straightened, his gaze riveted on Jackie's bedroom door. Eve shrank back, wondering if he'd spotted her through the crack. She heard the soft thud of his boots as he came toward her. She retreated to the closet, leaving the door ajar so she could track him if he came into her mother's room.

The footsteps stopped. A second later, he toed the door open, then stood on the threshold, one arm propped on the door frame as he surveyed his ex-wife's private domain. He took a long swig from the bottle, his gaze seemingly fixated on the bed. Then he meandered around the room much as he'd done in the den, drawing his hand along the top of the dresser, down one of the bedposts and across the linen duvet cover.

Returning to the dresser, he opened the top drawer and removed what looked to be one of Jackie's nightgowns. Holding the silky fabric against his face, he breathed in deeply before moving back to the bed.

Eve's skin crawled as she watched him. She wanted nothing so much as to kick open the closet door and scream at him to keep his hands off her mother's things, to get the hell out of her house and never come back. But she held back now because she needed to know what he was up to. How often did he come into her mother's home when she was gone and touch her things?

Setting his beer on one of the nightstands, he stretched out on top of the bed and propped his head on the pillows. Wrapping the nightgown around both hands, he snapped the fabric taut, as if testing the strength. Eve shivered as her hand crept to the dime beneath her shirt.

Taking out her phone, she snapped a photograph through the crack in the door. The click of the shutter sounded as loud as a rifle shot to Eve. She wasn't even sure she had him in focus, but she didn't want to risk giving herself away by taking another. Holding her breath, she waited for him to react to the sound. Engrossed in his own creepy thoughts, he remained seemingly oblivious to her presence.

Finally, he rose from the bed, fluffed the pillows and smoothed the impression of his body from the duvet cover. He picked up the beer bottle and wiped away the moisture from the nightstand with his sleeve. Then he returned the nightgown to the dresser drawer and left the room.

Eve trailed after him, watching from behind the bedroom door as he picked up the toolbox and disappeared down the hallway. He obviously hadn't come here to repair the leaky faucet or anything else. He'd brought his toolbox in case Jackie came home unexpectedly and caught him.

His behavior was beyond unsettling. Eve was shocked but not surprised. Not really. Maybe there was a reason she'd never warmed to Wayne Brody. Kids had good instincts about certain people. Maybe deep down she'd sensed something dark and disturbing behind his good-guy demeanor.

She'd have to tell her mother, of course. The sooner Jackie rid herself of Wayne Brody's presence in her life the better. But it might be a bitter pill for her to swallow. Jackie's first husband had left her for another woman. She'd always comforted herself with the knowledge that even though her marriage to Wayne hadn't worked out, she was capable of attracting someone loyal and decent. Someone who loved and adored her and wanted nothing more in the world than to care for her and her child.

Eve would have to find a way to break it to her gently, but break it to her she would. Her mother needed to know what kind of man Wayne Brody really was.

Of course, that would mean admitting to Jackie that Eve had also entered her house and gone through her things. That would mean she'd have to come clean about her suspicions regarding the identity of the skeletal remains. Jackie would be angry and hurt that Eve hadn't told her earlier, but she'd get over it. Their disagreements never lasted long.

Nash was a different story. He'd have every justification for taking the case away from her just when she was finally getting the answers she'd so desperately needed for years.

Checking both ways down the street for Wayne's truck, she returned to her car and lowered the window to allow heat to escape while she phoned her mother at work. Jackie answered on the first ring.

"Dr. Mercer's office."

"It's me, Mom."

"Evie? Why are you calling me on the office phone? You know I don't like to tie up the line with personal calls."

"I know, Mom, but I was afraid you wouldn't answer your cell."

Jackie was instantly alarmed. "What's wrong? Are you okay?"

Her anxious tone reminded Eve of Delia Middleton's earlier concern about her son. "Yes, I'm fine. I just wanted to check and see how you're feeling today. How's the hand?"

Get ready to relax and indulge with your **FREE BOOKS** and more!

Claim up to FOUR NEW BOOKS & TWO MYSTERY GIFTS – absolutely FREE!

Dear Reader,

We both know life can be difficult at times. That's why it's important to treat yourself so you can relax and recharge once in a while.

And I'd like to help you do this by sending you this amazing offer of up to FOUR brand new full length FREE BOOKS that WE pay for.

This is everything I have ready to send to you right now:

Try **Harlequin® Romantic Suspense** books featuring heart-racing page-turners with unexpected plot twists and irresistible chemistry that will keep you guessing to the very end.

Try **Harlequin Intrigue® Larger-Print** books featuring action-packed stories that will keep you on the edge of your seat. Solve the crime and deliver justice at all costs.

Or **TRY BOTH!**

All we ask in return is that you answer 4 simple questions on the attached Treat Yourself survey. You'll get **Two Free Books** and **Two Mystery Gifts** from each series you try, *altogether worth over $20!* Who could pass up a deal like that?

Sincerely,

Pam Powers

Harlequin Reader Service

Treat Yourself to Free Books and Free Gifts.

Answer 4 fun questions and get rewarded.

▼ DETACH AND MAIL CARD TODAY!

	YES	NO
1. I LOVE reading a good book.	○	○
2. I indulge and "treat" myself often.	○	○
3. I love getting FREE things.	○	○
4. Reading is one of my favorite activities.	○	○

TREAT YOURSELF • Pick your 2 Free Books...

Yes! Please send me my Free Books from each series I select and Free Mystery Gifts. I understand that I am under no obligation to buy anything, as explained on the back of this card.

Which do you prefer?

❑ **Harlequin® Romantic Suspense** 240/340 HDL GRCZ
❑ **Harlequin Intrigue® Larger-Print** 199/399 HDL GRCZ
❑ **Try Both** 240/340 & 199/399 HDL GRDD

FIRST NAME	LAST NAME

ADDRESS

APT.#	CITY

STATE/PROV.	ZIP/POSTAL CODE

EMAIL ❑ Please check this box if you would like to receive newsletters and promotional emails from Harlequin Enterprises ULC and its affiliates. You can unsubscribe anytime.

HI/HRS-520-TY22

"It hurts, but I'll live."

"I'm not surprised. That cut is deep. I thought I might come over later and do some chores for you. Whatever needs to be done, just name it. Maybe afterward we could talk."

Her mother hesitated. "That's sweet of you, Evie, and in a day or two I'll take you up on the offer. Today I just want to go home, take one of my pills and crawl into bed. It's been a long day. I'm exhausted and my head is throbbing."

"But you have to eat. I could bring dinner," Eve suggested.

"Wayne already offered, but I told him not to bother. If I get hungry I'll make some scrambled eggs and toast."

"Speaking of Wayne—"

"Don't start," her mother warned. "I'm not in the mood."

"But there's something you need to know."

Jackie held firm. "There is nothing I need to know that can't wait. I'm asking you to respect my wishes. Give me some space. Is that too much to ask?"

"No…"

"I'll call you tomorrow. We'll have dinner together soon, I promise. Right now I need to get back to work."

She hung up before Eve could utter another word, much less a proper goodbye. That wasn't like Jackie, but then, her mother's brush-off only added to Eve's growing list of strange behaviors in the people around her.

Someone rapped on the passenger-side window. Eve glanced around to find Wayne Brody peering in through the glass. How long had he been standing there and how much had he overheard?

Reluctantly, she lowered the window. He propped his forearms on the door and ducked his head to give her a curious stare. "I thought that was you. What are you doing parked all the way down here?"

"I pulled over to make a call," Eve lied. "Safety first."

His gaze dropped briefly to her holstered weapon. "Still on the job or are you headed home?"

Eve shrugged and forced a nonchalant tone. "Still on the job. I happened to be in the area, so I thought I'd drive by Mom's and see if she's home."

He looked skeptical. "It's the middle of the afternoon. You know she never leaves the office before five."

"I was hoping she'd knocked off early today."

"Why didn't you just call her to see if she's home?"

His interrogation irritated Eve. She was tempted to confront him with what she'd seen inside her mother's bedroom, but she wanted to talk to Jackie first. Why give Wayne the chance to come up with a plausible excuse, one that might leave Eve looking paranoid and vindictive in her mother's eyes? Jackie had always been strangely defensive when it came to Wayne Brody.

Eve scowled across the seat at him. "Not that I should have to explain myself to you, Wayne, but I already told you—I was in the area anyway. Now it's your turn. What are you doing here?"

His gaze was very direct, almost too intense. Did he know she'd been watching him? "I live in the neighborhood, remember?"

She nodded through the windshield. "Your house is down that way."

"I ran home for a late lunch and thought I'd fix that leaky faucet while I'm here. One less thing for Jackie to worry about."

"Did you check with her first?"

"Why would I do that? I know where she keeps the spare key. She told me a long time ago I could come and go as I needed to."

Eve's gaze narrowed. "How often is that?"

He cocked his head. "Can I ask you something? I'd like an honest answer. What's your problem with me?"

"Who said I had a problem?"

He grinned. "You've never made any bones about it. When Jackie and me got married, you were just a little kid. I could understand your bratty behavior back then. You didn't like the idea of someone taking your daddy's place, let alone sharing your mama. But you're a grown woman now, Evie."

"Don't call me that."

"Maybe you should get your own life, *Eve*, and quit sticking your nose in your mama's personal business."

"Maybe you should take your own advice," Eve shot back. "Stop hanging around my mother and hoping for something that's never going to happen."

His tone remained amiable, but his gaze hardened. "You don't know anything about me. Or Jackie, either, for that matter. You think you know her, but you don't. Not like I do."

"What's that supposed to mean?" Eve demanded.

"Jackie and I share a bond that even you can't break, though God knows you've tried. We have history."

"Yes, and there's a divorce in that history, in case you forgot."

He gave her a knowing look. "It kills you that we're still friends, doesn't it? More than friends. I would do anything for her and she knows it. Unlike Gabriel Jareau."

Eve gripped the edge of the car seat. "Leave him out of this."

"Why? Because you still want to believe he was someone special? I get that," Wayne said. "Your daddy had a way about him. Everybody liked him. But when you got past his smile and all that smooth talk, he was just a petty criminal like all his buddies. You ever ask yourself what kind of man turns his back on his own child?"

Yes, Eve thought. *Every day since I was five years old.*

"You ever ask yourself why he up and left the way he did? What he might have been running from?"

Eve's voice rose sharply. "What are you talking about?"

Wayne hesitated, as if on the verge of revealing some deep, dark secret about her father. Then he said with an enigmatic smile, "You really have no idea what he was capable of, do you?"

Chapter Eight

Eve couldn't stop thinking about the confrontation with Wayne Brody and the implication that her dad had been mixed up in something illegal. That should have come as no surprise. She'd always suspected he and his companions had been up to no good that night. As much as she hated to admit it, Wayne was right about one thing. There must have been a reason her father had left town the way he had.

Wayne was certainly no innocent, either. His creepy little visit to her mother's bedroom was beyond disturbing. Eve had never considered him dangerous and even now, she was hard pressed to imagine him a physical threat to Jackie. But she couldn't know that for certain. She had to find a way to warn her mother without putting her on the defensive. She had to get to Jackie before Wayne could somehow spin the situation in his favor. Eve had learned years ago never to underestimate her ex-stepfather and the inexplicable connection he shared with her mother.

As she settled in at her desk, she tried to put Wayne Brody out of her head and immerse herself in the John

Doe case. It was a relief when Nash called her into his office late that afternoon to go over their notes. Even then, her mind kept wandering until Nash finally tossed his pen onto the desk and closed his notebook.

"What's up?"

Eve answered absently. "What?"

"You're distracted. You've barely said two words since we started."

"I'm sorry." Eve tried to shake off her mood. "I'm worried about my mom. She cut her hand last night, and I'm afraid the injury may be more serious than we first thought. I talked to her a little while ago and she seems to be in quite a bit of pain."

"I'm sorry to hear that," Nash said. "Has she seen a doctor?"

"Yes. Her ex-husband drove her to the ER last night."

Nash lifted a brow. "Her ex-husband?"

Eve made a face. "Wayne Brody. They've remained close since the divorce."

"And you don't approve?"

"Wayne is…" She struggled for the right word to convey her concern and disgust. "No. I don't approve."

Nash settled back in his chair, willing to listen. "How long ago did they split up?"

"Over twenty years ago."

He looked amazed. "And they've managed to remain friends all that time?"

"Unfortunately, yes."

He tilted his head as he took in her expression. "Why don't you like him?"

Eve wanted to tell him what she'd witnessed earlier

at her mother's home, but bringing personal problems into the workplace was never a good idea, so she tried to sum up her concern as succinctly as possible. "I don't trust him. I don't believe he's the kind of man he pretends to be. I think he's carried a torch for my mother all these years and he'll do anything to ingratiate himself with her." She stopped short and took a breath. "But that's more information than you ever needed to know about Wayne Brody. Let's get back to our notes. I promise you'll have my undivided attention from now on."

"I think we've pretty much covered everything. Unless you have something you want to add."

"No, I'm good."

He straightened and shuffled some papers on his desk. "Then take off. Go see your mother."

"I appreciate the offer, but she won't be home from work yet. Besides, I've still got reports to file."

"The reports will keep until morning. Go home, Eve. Come back in the morning with a fresh prospective."

She was tempted to do just that, but once she got back to her desk and saw the stack of reports waiting to be completed and filed, she decided to dig in for a bit. As usual, she lost track of time. When her stomach grumbled, she finally pushed away from the desk, stretched and collected her things from her locker before heading out.

Once at home she went through her regular routine of sorting through the mail and searching through the fridge for something to eat. Then she took a long shower, put on some comfortable shorts and her favorite T-shirt and went out to the backyard to relax.

The freshly mown grass tickled her bare feet as she walked across the lawn to the old swing suspended from a tree branch with chains. Settling herself on the cushions, she folded one leg beneath her while gently toeing the swing back and forth. She sat for the longest time watching the light fade as twilight crept in. Her garden grew shadowy and redolent. She thought about calling her mother, but Jackie had made it clear she wanted the evening to herself. Fair enough. She'd been through a lot, but Eve couldn't help wondering if her mother's insistence on being alone was a pretext to avoid more questions about Eve's dad.

The scent of the angel's trumpet against the fence hung heavy on the evening air, triggering a powerful melancholy. Eve found herself thinking again of the night her dad left as she drew the coin from her neckline and caressed the cool metal between her fingers.

Someone's coming, Boo.

Which had come first? she later wondered. Her father's phantom warning or the telltale squeak of her garden gate?

She tensed, her head whipping toward the sound as a figure materialized in the dusk. Instantly, she thought of the Glock in her nightstand drawer. Then she flashed to Wayne Brody pawing through her mother's private things and his subtle taunt that she knew nothing of the bond they shared, nothing of the crimes her father had committed before he left town.

"Who's there?" she called out.

"It's me."

Her heart tripped at the sound of Nash's voice even

as she experienced a sharp sense of relief that her ex-stepfather hadn't come calling.

Nash had never been to her house before. How did he even know where she lived?

And how disconcerting to see him striding so surely across her shadowy backyard as if he'd been there many times before.

All this went through her mind in the blink of an eye as he approached. He still wore the clothes he'd had on earlier, so Eve figured he'd come straight from the station.

"Don't get up," he said when she started to rise. "I hope it's all right that I stopped by without calling first. I rang the doorbell, but I guess you didn't hear it."

She dropped back down on the cushions. "How did you know to look for me out here?"

"I heard you mention once that you spend most of your evenings in the garden." He glanced around at the lush vegetation. "I can see why. This must take an awful lot of work."

Eve tucked the dime back into her neckline. "Most of it was planted before I moved in, but I like to putter around out here and pretend I know what I'm doing. I actually enjoy pulling weeds. It's mindless but productive." *You're rambling, Eve. Just shut up.* She paused to stare up at him. "Why are you here?"

"I thought we should talk."

That either sounded ominous or promising, but Eve allowed nothing more than mild curiosity to seep into her voice. "About the John Doe case?"

His slight hesitation sent a shiver up her spine. "Yes."

"Would you rather talk inside?" Would that be more or less nerve-racking? she wondered. "It's still pretty warm out here and the mosquitos will be bad now that it's getting on dark."

"No, I like the fresh air. I've been cooped up in the office for hours." He canted his head and drew a long breath. "What's that scent?"

"Angel's trumpet. It blooms all summer long. Sometimes the fragrance can be a bit overpowering in the heat." There she was, rambling again. Small talk had never been her strong suit, especially when caught off guard. Even less so when it came to Nash Bowden. Why was he really here?

"Angel's trumpet," he murmured. "Is that the one with the big bell-shaped flowers? My grandmother grew it in her garden. She had a little place in Franklin County near the Gulf. I spent every summer there until I joined the army." His tone subtly altered. "Seems like a lifetime ago now."

Nash had never been one to share his personal life with his colleagues. This glimpse into his past mesmerized Eve. She drew up her legs and wrapped her arms around her knees. "Are you and your grandmother still close?"

"She passed away while I was stationed overseas."

"I'm sorry."

He shrugged. "No need to be sorry. She lived a long, happy life and then went peacefully in her sleep. That scent took me back to her for a moment."

"Do you want to sit?" She unfolded her legs and scooted over to make room for him on the swing. He sat down beside her, brushing up against her bare thigh. Another thrill shot through her. She tugged on the cuff of her shorts and told herself to relax. She'd been in Nash's company all day long. This was no different. But somehow being here with him in her fragrant garden seemed too familiar, almost unbearably intimate.

Could he tell she was nervous? Could he sense the flutter in her stomach and the sudden rush of adrenaline through her veins? Her face felt flushed. Could he see that, too? She'd tried so hard to keep her emotions in check ever since that ill-conceived kiss, but they were sitting so close and tonight he seemed so vulnerable and approachable. She wondered what had brought on his reflective mood.

"The autopsy is scheduled for seven in the morning," he said, dousing the heat of her attraction with a splash of cold reality.

"Oh. Okay. That's pretty early."

"There's really no need in both of us attending," he said.

She gave him a pointed glance. "Are you volunteering?"

"If you've no objection."

"You don't need my permission, obviously, but that's fine by me. I've never gotten used to autopsies."

"No one does. I'll let you know if anything interesting turns up." He curled his fingers around the chain and used his feet to rock them to and fro. They swung in amiable silence for a moment, their faces tipped to the breeze. The perfume from the flowers deepened, lingering in the senses like a memory. In such a dreamy setting, it seemed almost obscene to discuss murder, but they were both cops and there was an old homicide and possibly a fresh one still to solve.

"Any news on the Nadine Crosby front?" she asked.

"Not yet. Have you heard anything?"

She tucked back a loose strand of hair. "I plan to talk to Delia Middleton again tomorrow. She may have remembered something now that the initial shock of finding us in her office has worn off. I'd also like to speak with some of the other employees. Maybe one of them knows something about Nadine's whereabouts."

"Let me know what you find out."

She nodded, staring straight ahead, but she could see him from her periphery, knew that his eyes were on her, too. *This is so strange*, she thought. Disconcerting and titillating all at the same time.

"How's your mom?" he asked. "You seemed really worried about her this afternoon."

"I'm still worried. I haven't seen her today, but when I called earlier, she said she wanted to take a pain pill and go to bed. I'm trying to respect her wishes, but it's hard because I need to talk to her about something important and it could drive a wedge between us if I'm not careful."

"That's a tough one," he said. "Does it have something to do with the ex-husband you mentioned earlier?"

Eve nodded. "I found out something upsetting about Wayne, but she always gets defensive when I bring him up. It's like he has some kind of weird hold on her."

"Are you sure it's something she needs to know?"

Eve turned and met his gaze in the twilight. "I caught

him in her house earlier going through some of her personal things. It makes me wonder how often he's done that in the twenty years since they split. Then he laid on her bed and garroted the air with her nightgown."

"He what?"

She simulated Wayne's disturbing action. "I've never thought of him as dangerous, but his behavior is troublesome, to say the least."

"That is troublesome," Nash agreed. "Sometimes it only takes the smallest trigger to set someone off."

Was he thinking about his own situation with Grace? What had prompted her to abduct little Kylie Buchanan? Had she been trying to fill a void or to get Nash's attention?

"Then you think I should tell her?" Eve asked.

"I think you have to."

It was such a relief to confide in someone, but she had no right dropping that burden on Nash. Grace's court date was coming up soon. He had more than enough on his plate without taking on Eve's problems. "I'm sorry. I didn't mean to get into all that again. You didn't come over here to listen to my problems."

"I wouldn't have asked if I didn't care." He stretched his arm along the back of the swing. "Tell me more about this guy. You said he and your mom have been divorced for over twenty years. He never remarried?"

"I doubt he even dates," Eve said. "He bought a house down the street from my mom's so he can be at her beck and call night and day. That's not normal, right? It's not just me."

"It sounds a little codependent," Nash said.

"Yes, and my mom only encourages him by using him as her private handyman. The least little thing goes wrong and she calls Wayne to come over and fix it."

"Maybe she still has feelings for him, too," Nash suggested.

Eve winced. "Bite your tongue. To be honest, I don't think she ever got over my dad. If I were to ask her, she'd deny any lingering feelings, but she gets this far-away look in her eyes whenever he's mentioned. He was her first love. They were high school sweethearts although they didn't marry until my mom turned twenty-one."

"Is your dad still in the picture?"

Eve tensed. *Yes, I think he might be.*

Now would be the perfect time to come clean about her suspicions regarding John Doe's identity. Confess everything and let the chips fall where they may. Maybe Nash would surprise her and allow her to remain on the case. But he had protocol to follow and Eve wasn't willing to take the chance he'd make an exception. Not when she'd just learned the identity of her father's companions, possibly his killers. Assuming, of course, the skeletal remains were his.

"He left when I was five," Eve said. "He took off one night and never came back."

"You never heard from him again?"

"He sent a few postcards to me and some money to my mom, but he never called or tried to see me. Mom always believed he left us for someone else. Another woman. I guess his new love was the only family he wanted or needed."

"That must have been hard on you, losing your dad like that."

"I adored him. For him to just up and leave us… It was devastating." Nash's arm was still draped along the back of the swing. Eve resisted the urge to lay her head against him. "That was the same summer Maya Lamb went missing. She was only a little bit younger than me and she didn't have a father to protect her, either. For the longest time, I was terrified that her kidnapper would come in through my bedroom window one night and take me, too."

"You weren't the only one with that fear," Nash said. "I talked to a lot of people about Maya's abduction after Kylie Buchanan went missing, when we still thought there might be a link. My impression is that the town never got over Maya's kidnapping. Twenty-eight years after Maya disappeared, a shadow still hovers over Black Creek. Maybe that's why Grace was able to convince even law enforcement that the same person who abducted Maya also took Kylie. We were predisposed to look for that connection."

His eyes gleamed darkly in the moonlight. Eve could sense his warmth, could almost hear his heartbeat. He'd never talked to her so openly about his ex-wife's heinous crime and Eve had never felt so close to him as she did at that moment.

"Grace knew intimate details of Maya's kidnapping because, like me, she's lived in Black Creek for most of her life," Eve said. "As a child, she even became friends with Maya's twin sister, Thea. That surely made an impact on her. Years later, she used everything she'd learned from Thea, everything she'd taken from their home when she decided to abduct Kylie Buchanan. I'll say it again, Nash. She was very clever. No one could have seen that coming."

He was silent for a moment. "You're right. She is very clever. Which is why I think it's a mistake for you to talk to her."

"I know you do, but she may not agree to see me anyway. The subject could be moot."

"She'll see you."

Eve could hear the tension in his voice. "How do you know?"

"Because I know her. The chance to garner empathy from someone who works closely with me would be irresistible to her."

"I don't empathize with her."

"Not yet."

Eve's hackles rose in defense. "Give me a little credit. I know how to handle myself."

He looked as if he wanted to argue that point, but then he conceded. "Sorry. I have a tendency to overreact when it comes to Grace. I know you can handle yourself. I wouldn't be here otherwise."

"What do you mean?"

He stopped the swing with his foot. Everything suddenly seemed a little too quiet in the garden. "A forensic psychiatrist named Linda Anderson called the station earlier to set up a time for your visit."

Eve turned in surprise, searching his profile in the dusk. "Why contact you? I'm the one who made the request."

"She needed to confirm you'd gone through the proper channels. It's complicated with Grace's hearing coming up. Her attorneys also had to sign off on the visit. They've limited your time and the scope of the interview. You won't be allowed to ask questions about Kylie Buchanan's kidnapping."

"I understand."

"The meeting will be video recorded so you'll need to keep the focus on the John Doe case. It's imperative you not give Grace anything that she and her attorneys can use in court."

"When can I see her?" Eve was suddenly nervous about the prospect.

"Tomorrow morning, nine o'clock sharp. Dr. Anderson will make all the necessary arrangements. An escort will meet you at the metal detectors and take you back."

"That soon?" Eve had thought she might have a day or two to prepare.

"I suspect Grace had a hand in the timing. Her immediate need for attention undoubtedly overcame her desire to have me stew for several days about what she might be up to."

"I'm sorry this is so hard for you," Eve said. "If there was any other way—"

"Don't worry about me. I'm fine." He didn't sound so fine.

"You don't need to worry about me, either. I'll make sure I'm at the hospital on time and I'll be careful what I say to her. I'm guessing that's why you're here, isn't it? You could have told me about the autopsy over the phone. You were hoping you could talk me out of going to see her."

"Yes," he replied candidly. "I didn't think it would work, but I had to try."

"You're really that concerned?"

"She'll have an agenda," he warned. "She always does."

"And yet you married her." The comment slipped out before she could stop herself, but she really didn't regret her bluntness. She'd wondered for years how such an ill-fated match had come about. *But look at Mom and Wayne Brody.* People married for all kinds of reasons. She still didn't understand why or how her mother could have succumbed to Wayne's charmless courtship. Had she been that lonely after Eve's dad split?

"I married her because she saved my life," Nash said. "But that's a long story and I think Grace has occupied too much of our time as it is."

Was he talking about tonight or the past six years? Eve ran a hand up her bare arm, where goose bumps had risen despite the steamy heat. Had his fingers brushed against her hair or was that merely her imagination?

He glanced out over the garden toward the house. "I've always wondered about where you live," he said unexpectedly.

She swallowed. "You have?"

"Sometimes I've tried to picture you out here in your garden."

Eve had no idea what to say to that. The low rumble of his baritone voice in the dark made all those goose bumps tingle with awareness. "My childhood home is a few blocks from here. My mother still lives in the same house where I grew up."

"It's a nice neighborhood. I like all the trees." Was that a note of disappointment in his voice? Had he wanted the conversation to go in a different direction? It would be up to him to steer her back, Eve decided. She'd made the first move once and the humiliation still lingered, despite the intensity of his response.

"It's been just my mom and me for most of my life," she said. "When I left for college, it was the first time we'd spent more than a night apart."

"Is that why you came back to Black Creek? To be near her?"

"I lived in Tallahassee for a while after I graduated. It never felt like home."

"I get it," he said. "Roots are important. Or so I'm told."

She turned at that strange edge in his voice. "What about you? Where did you grow up?"

"My dad was in the military so we lived all over the place. Spending summers with my grandmother was the closest thing I had to roots."

How crazy that Eve had worked with him all these years, had dreamed about him more often than she would ever admit, and she was just now coming to know him. She wasn't sure what to make of his visit, much less his openness. If he was about to make his move, why now when she was keeping a secret from him?

As if sensing her hesitancy he said, "I should go. I've interrupted your evening for far too long." He rose. "I'll see you tomorrow."

She untucked her legs and stood. "I'll let you know when I get back from Tallahassee."

He stared down at her in the darkness. "You know what I'm thinking so I'm not going to say it."

Eve tipped her head so that she could meet his gaze. "You don't need to worry about me. I'll be careful."

"That wasn't what I was thinking."

He reached out, cupping the back of her neck to pull her to him. Eve tried to brace herself, tried to summon the willpower and common sense to send him away. She said breathlessly, "Nash, what are you doing?"

"What I've wanted to do all day. What I've wanted to do for years. I can't stop thinking about you, Eve."

As much as she wanted to melt into him, she couldn't. Not yet. Not until there was complete honesty between them. Not when he needed to protect himself. "We can't do this. Once Grace's psychiatric evaluations are completed, a date will be set for the competency hearing. You have to be careful about appearances."

"Grace and I are divorced. I don't owe her anything."

"I know, but her attorneys will be looking for any angle to present her as a sympathetic victim. You're the ex-husband. They'll try every trick in the book to turn you into the villain, to make it seem as though you're the one who pushed her over the edge. You have to do everything you can to protect yourself."

"By protecting myself, I'm allowing her to manipulate me."

"It's not the same thing," Eve insisted. "You've warned me over and over to be careful with Grace. Now I'm asking you to do the same."

He pulled her to him anyway, but instead of kissing her, he rested his forehead against hers. It was a tender moment. A vulnerable gesture that further eroded Eve's defenses.

She closed her eyes, drawing in the scent of him and the radiating warmth of his nearness. She still wanted him, but now she also wanted to know him, to protect him. To give him strength in the stressful days that lay ahead of him. In the space of one evening, her feelings for Nash Bowden had deepened profoundly.

Finally he pulled away and took her hand. She walked him to the back gate, where they said goodnight and parted. She stood listening for his ignition and only when the sound of his engine faded into the night did she close the gate and go inside.

Eve had the strangest dream that night. She was back at her bedroom window staring down at her father as he climbed into the front seat beside Nadine Crosby. But when the figure in the back seat glanced up at her, Denton Crosby's nebulous features morphed into Wayne Brody's. He grinned, lifting a finger to his lips and then across his throat.

She awakened in a cold sweat, unsure of whether a noise or the dream had roused her. Staring up at the ceiling, she willed herself back to a calmer place before another sound catapulted her upright in bed. She reached for her weapon as she rose, then padded to the window to glance out at the garden.

Searching through the shadows, she let her gaze rest for a moment on the back-and-forth movement of the swing. Had the rattle of the chains awakened her? There was only a mild breeze, not enough to set the swing in motion. Someone was out there. She knew it with a certainty that bordered on premonition.

Be careful, Boo.

She glanced over her shoulder, almost expecting to find a silhouette lurking in a corner of her bedroom. She swept the room and then turned back to the window. She could see someone in the shadows just beyond the swing. The same interloper she'd spied outside her bedroom window all those years ago? Or was she imagining an intruder?

Hiding behind the linen curtains, she watched the shadow for another moment and then slipped across the room and out into the hallway. She didn't turn on the light. Moonlight shimmering in through the windows guided her through the silent house. She paused at the back door to peer through the glass panel. Then she let herself out, closing the door behind her with a soft click. She hid among the trees and bushes, maneuvering soundlessly through the vegetation so that she could come up behind the swing. If someone was there, she hoped to catch him unawares.

The breeze lifted her hair and teased through the thin cotton of her pajamas. Eve pressed the Glock against her thigh, trying to convince herself she'd overreacted to a shadow even as her instincts warned of danger. A cloud passed over the moon, throwing the yard into pitch-blackness. Somewhere behind her, she heard the telltale snap of a twig. She whirled, shifting her weight automatically as she lifted her weapon. "Who's there?"

"Evie?"

She drew a sharp breath. For one paralyzing moment, she could have sworn Gabriel Jareau had returned from the dead—or from wherever he'd been the past twenty-eight years. In the next instant, the visitor laughed, a low, menacing sound that prickled the hair at the back of her neck.

"Who are you?" The laugh had come from her left. She turned toward the sound. "Come out where I can see you."

"I can't do that, Evie."

She used both hands to steady her weapon. "Show yourself."

"It's been a long time. You wouldn't recognize me, kiddo. But I'd know you anywhere."

"You're not my dad."

"Never said I was."

She braced her stance. "I know who you are. Your name is Denton Crosby. You were with my dad the night he left town. You and your sister, Nadine." Eve spotted a dark silhouette hovering under the oak tree. But when he spoke again, the voice came from another area of the yard. How could he creep so seamlessly through her garden? Was he, too, a ghost or did he have a companion? His sister, perhaps?

Eve thought about all those times as a child when she'd awakened in the middle of the night with the spine-tingling certainty of being watched. She'd wanted to believe her father had come back to keep her safe from Maya Lamb's kidnapper, but she'd never been able to justify the feeling of malignancy that had radiated from the unknown watcher. It was the same malice that enveloped her now as she searched the shadows.

"So you know who I am." He spoke with a note of regret. "I really wish you'd left well enough alone, Evie. Your knowing my name complicates things."

"Murder is always complicated." She tracked the sound of his voice, turning her head slowly as her gaze raked the darkness. "Is that why you killed Ron Naples? Did he complicate things?"

"Who?"

"He was an old man. Surely not a threat to someone like you. What happened? Did he catch you stealing his car? Or was your sister the one who pushed him into the river?"

"You don't know what you're talking about. You have no idea about any of this."

"I know more than you think," she countered. "I saw you in the car waiting for my dad the night he left town. I can place you in his company. Only he didn't leave town, did he? You and Nadine killed him. When you heard about the discovery of the remains in the cave, you were afraid I'd remember. So you took Ron Naples's car and tried to run me down on the highway, hoping the police wouldn't be able to trace the incident back to you."

"You think you've got it all figured out, don't you? Gabriel always said you were too smart for your own good." The disembodied voice taunted her, though Eve liked to think there was worry in his tone.

She inched around a tree. "You killed my dad and buried him down in that cavern, hoping his body would never be found."

"Evie, Evie. If you only knew the can of worms you're about to open."

He was behind her now. Eve sensed his presence a split second too late. A hand clapped over her mouth, pulling her back against a muscular body as the barrel of a gun pressed against the base of her skull. "Drop your weapon." When Eve resisted, he pulled the hammer back on his revolver. "I said, drop it."

She let the Glock fall to the ground.

"Kick it behind you."

Again she did as she was told.

He booted the gun into the bushes before he removed his hand from her mouth. "Don't even think about screaming."

She said over her shoulder, "What do you want?"

His warm breath fanned against her neck as he brought his lips close to her ear. "Listen carefully. What happened down in that cave needs to stay buried."

"It's too late for that."

"No, it's not. A smart girl like you can still fix things. Drop the investigation and no one else has to get hurt."

She swallowed back her fear, certain now that Denton Crosby had entered Nash's home and looked through the John Doe files. How else would he know that she'd been assigned to the case? He'd been one step ahead of her ever since the remains had been recovered. "I don't have the authority to drop an investigation," she told him.

"That's not what I hear. You're in charge, aren't you? Leads dry up and evidence goes missing all the time. If you know what's good for you and yours, you'll find a way."

Eve half turned, trying to catch a glimpse of his features. "Is that a threat?"

"It's a fact." He poked her in the back with the gun barrel. "Now face straight ahead and don't try that again. I don't want to hurt you out of respect for my old friend, but I will if I have to."

"Don't want to hurt me," she repeated incredulously. "You tried to run me down with a stolen car."

"If I'd wanted you dead out on that highway, you'd be lying in a morgue right now. I only meant to prove what an easy target you are. I can get to you whenever I want. I always could. You'd best remember that. Now put your hands behind your back where I can see them."

She clasped her hands against the base of her spine. "Why don't you want me to see your face? I already know who you are."

"You don't know half as much as you think you do." He nudged her again with the revolver. "You need to understand something. This isn't just about Nadine and me."

"Who else is involved?"

"Oh, I can give you an earful if you're willing to listen. How about we start with that sweet mama of yours?"

An icy chill swept down Eve's backbone. "Leave her out of this."

"I can't do that, Evie. You want the truth, don't you? Well, here's a hard one for you, kiddo. I've known Jackie since high school. That girl was always a looker. A real heartbreaker. Had a little crush on her myself back in the day. But she was never as high and mighty as she pretended to be. You think she didn't know what Gabriel was up to all those nights he didn't come home? You think she didn't suspect what he had planned *that* night?"

Eve's heart thudded. "What are you talking about?"

"She knew all along the kind of man she married. A lot of women are attracted to danger, but some just don't want to admit it."

"Stop talking about my mother as if you know her," Eve snapped. "You don't know anything about her."

"I know plenty. More than you could ever imagine. Gabriel Jareau was my best friend. The two of us were like brothers. He told me things about his wife he never told another living soul."

Eve wasn't about to let the likes of Denton Crosby speak ill of her mother. But even as her defenses hardened, she wondered if a small part of her was afraid to hear any more of his accusations. "As if I would believe anything coming out of your mouth. If you're planning on killing me tonight, why don't you just get on with it? Your blathering on this way is starting to wear on my last nerve."

He laughed. "You know what? You sounded an awful lot like your old man just then." His humor faded and his voice deepened. "Gabriel always did have a tendency to pop off when he should have kept his trap shut and listened. Maybe he'd still be alive."

Eve's nails dug into her palms. "Is that a confession?"

"I said *listen*. You know what Jackie told Gabriel before he left her? She said she'd kill him if he ever tried to come back. Shoot him straight through the heart if he ever tried to call or see you again."

"That's a lie," Eve said even as her mind raced back to those postcards and the discrepancy she'd noted in the handwriting. She didn't believe for a moment that her mother had forged her father's handwriting to prove he was still alive, but someone had. She was more convinced than ever that Gabriel Jareau had been long dead when the last postcard had been sent.

"You expect me to take your word for any of this?" she demanded. "You know what I think? You're trying to deflect guilt onto my mother when you're the one who killed my dad. You lured him down into that cave and ambushed him. What I don't understand is why. You said he was your friend."

"I said he was like a brother to me. Why would I want to hurt him?"

"Then why do you care about the John Doe investigation? Unless…my father wasn't the one buried in that grave. Unless you're trying to protect someone else."

"*Listen* to me. I'm only going to say this one more time. I could have silenced you a long time ago if I'd been of the mind to. I could have shot you in the back tonight and saved myself a lot of grief, but I decided to try to talk some sense into you instead. I don't want to hurt you, but you can't be running around all over town yapping about what you think you know. You keep going down the path you're on and it won't only be me that ends up in prison. How long do you think your mama would last in a place like Lowell? That hellhole just about killed my sister and she's as tough as they come. What do you think it would do to a woman like Jackie?"

"Nadine was in prison?"

He ignored the question. "Ask her about the last time she saw your daddy alive. Ask her why she wouldn't let him come inside the house to see you the night he snuck back into town."

Eve half turned. "He came back?"

"Of course he came back. He thought the sun rose and set on you. Maybe that was the last straw for Jackie after he up and left the way he did. Maybe she made good on her threat and somehow got him to meet her down in the cave."

"That doesn't make any sense. Why on earth would she lure him to the cave? The tunnels are difficult to navigate even if you know what you're doing."

"Oh, she knew what she was doing, all right. Jackie knew that cave like the back of her hand. We all did. That was our place back in the day, but I'm guessing she never told you any of that. I'm guessing she's gotten real good at keeping secrets. You might want to ask yourself what else she's been hiding before you keep trying to dig up the past."

Chapter Nine

The next morning, Eve made a quick detour to Dr. Forester's lab before heading over to the hospital for her interview with Grace Bowden. The forensic anthropologist was curious about the anonymous DNA swab Eve dropped off, but she agreed to run the test discreetly and let Eve know as soon as the results came back.

She pulled the dime from her collar and caressed the metal between her thumb and forefinger before getting out of the car at the hospital. *I'm getting close to the truth, Daddy.*

Careful what you wish for, Boo.

Shivering despite the heat, she let her gaze roam over the austere brick-and-glass facade as she thought back over the events of the past two days. She hadn't known it at the time, but her life had changed the moment those bones had been discovered. When Nash had offered her lead on the investigation, she'd naively been excited and intrigued by the prospect of working a cold case on her own terms. But that was before she'd learned of the holed coin that had been found at the burial site. That was before her mother had reacted so strongly to Eve's questions about her dad, before Denton Crosby had made his wild accusations in her garden. *I'm guessing she's gotten real good at keeping secrets. You might want to ask yourself what else she's been hiding before you keep trying to dig up the past.*

Eve closed her eyes and took a calming breath. Whatever else she uncovered in the course of her investigation, she'd soon know the truth about John Doe's identity. If the DNA tests turned up a familial match, she'd have to reveal the results to Nash, and then he'd have no choice but to remove her from the case. She'd already forced his hand by going behind his back.

No matter his decision, though, she couldn't just walk away. She couldn't allow Denton Crosby's accusations about her mother to dangle forever at the back of her mind. She had to find out what happened down in that cave all those years ago even if it cost her a job she loved and the trust of a man she admired. Even if it led her down a path she might end up regretting forever.

Shaking herself out of a dark reverie, she let the dime drop back into her collar as she steadied her pulse and refocused. Time enough to worry about the consequences of her actions later. Right now she had to prepare for the interview with Grace. If Nash's ex-wife was half as cunning and clever as he made her out to be, Eve couldn't afford to let her guard down even for a second.

Upon entering the psychiatric wing, she signed in and surrendered her weapon before going through the metal detector. Then she was led down a hallway to a small windowless space that reminded her of the interrogation room at the station. The attendant ushered her in and left. She noted the cameras mounted in two corners before seating herself at the table facing the only entrance. A few minutes later, the same attendant opened the door and stood aside for Grace Bowden to enter. He nodded to Eve and told her if she needed anything he'd be right outside.

Grace stood for a moment, taking in the room before she crossed to the table and sat down opposite Eve. They'd briefly met once when Grace had come into the station and a second time when Eve had stopped in at Grace's antique doll store looking for a gift. That was before she and Nash had had their moment, although he and Grace had been long separated by that time. Eve couldn't remember now what she and Grace had talked about. The dolls had been out of her price range so she'd browsed for only a few minutes and then left.

She tried to keep her expression courteous but guarded as she took in Grace's appearance. She was dressed in jeans, sneakers and a light blue cardigan that she tugged around her body as she settled in at the table. The street attire surprised Eve. *What were you expecting? A straitjacket?*

Grace's dark blond hair was pulled back and braided, her eyes slightly dilated, making Eve wonder if she'd been sedated. Eve tried to picture Nash and Grace together, but she couldn't make herself go there.

As if to mock her denial, the gold wedding band on Grace's left ring finger gleamed in the overhead lighting as she folded her hands on the table. "So you're Eve Jareau. You're older than I thought you'd be."

Eve decided not to take the observation as a slight seeing as how she and Grace were close to the same age. "We've met before," she said. "Do you remember?"

Grace took a moment to think back then shook her head. "No, I'm sorry. I can't seem to place you. But I grew up in Black Creek so it's likely our paths have crossed more than once. We may even have gone to the same school."

"Very likely," Eve agreed.

"They said you're a homicide detective with the Black Creek Police Department. That means you work with my husband."

Had she stressed the last word or had Eve imagined the emphasis? "I'm with the criminal investigations unit so I work on all kinds of major crimes. Cold cases are of particular interest to me."

Grace sat forward, her previously hooded eyes now curious and alert. "Really? Because I'm fascinated by old crimes, too. Take the Maya Lamb kidnapping case. She was taken right here in Black Creek, right in my own backyard, so to speak. That alone would have captured my interest, but there were so many holes in her mother's story, so many loose ends that never got tied up. Nash says that's one case that may never be solved."

How casually and intimately she spoke of her ex-husband, as if they'd had a conversation about Maya Lamb over dinner the evening before. Eve wanted to explore Grace's fascination with the Lamb case and ask about the details from that crime that she'd incorporated into the kidnapping of Kylie Buchanan. But she had a feeling that was exactly Grace's intent, to steer her into the forbidden territory of Kylie's abduction.

She said carefully, "He could be right, but I hope not. Maya's family deserves to know what happened to her."

"Oh, yes, her family," Grace said dismissively. She gave Eve an unabashed appraisal. "Nash always speaks so highly of his detectives. I'm surprised he never mentioned you."

Was that meant as another slight? Had Grace somehow intuited Eve's feelings for Nash and was trying to get in a few digs? The notion made Eve distinctly uncomfortable. "I'm sure he has more important things on his mind." She summoned a professional briskness to her tone. "Anyway, thank you for agreeing to see me. I'm here because I thought you might be of help on one of my cases."

Grace nodded. "Another cold case, I'm told."

"Yes, a homicide. I'd like to talk to you about the skeletal remains that were discovered in McNally's Cave a few days ago. We've yet to identify the victim, but we do know he was murdered."

"He?"

"The victim was a tall white male, probably in his late twenties."

One brow lifted in puzzlement. "And you think I know something about his murder?"

"Not the murder, per se," Eve explained. "You said in your statement that you'd known about the burial site in the cavern since you were a child. You used to visit the grave because you thought Maya Lamb was buried there."

"It always comes back to Maya, doesn't it?" Grace's voice turned plaintive, her eyes dreamy and sad. "That kidnapping changed us all. People our age grew up knowing what happened to her could happen to any of us. That gnawing fear tainted our childhoods in ways we may never understand."

Eve felt a prickle of apprehension at the base of her spine. Was Grace trying to establish a sympathetic rapport by playing on their common history? That Eve had had a similar conversation the evening before with Nash only deepened her trepidation. No way Grace could have known about his visit, let alone their discussion concerning Maya Lamb's kidnapping, but she'd obviously tapped into an emotional tell that Eve had failed to suppress. The woman's insight and instincts bordered on the uncanny. Eve was beginning to understand Nash's dire warnings.

"Let's get back to that grave," she suggested. "Why did you think Maya was buried there?"

Grace shrugged. "As I said, Maya's kidnapping made a huge impact on me. She was the only one I knew of in town who'd gone missing, so it seemed a logical assumption at the time."

"Yet you never told anyone about your find. Not the authorities. Not even Maya's mother or sister." Eve tried not to sound judgmental, but a faint note of censure crept into her tone despite her best efforts.

Grace tugged the sweater around her slim body as if she could somehow ward off Eve's disapproval. "I was just a little kid. Besides, everybody in town knew what kind of mother Reggie Lamb was. She left her children alone at night while she partied with her degenerate friends. She let lowlifes stay in the same house where those little girls slept. God only knows what went on once she passed out. If she'd been sober the night Maya got taken, she could have protected her daughter. That's the most important job a mother has—to keep her children safe. Don't you agree, Detective Jareau?"

"Yes, if she's able." Too late, Eve recognized the woman's trap. Grace now claimed she'd kidnapped Kylie Buchanan to remove her from an abusive situation with her father. Eve had unwittingly skirted a little too close to sanctioning her motive.

"Maybe I felt so much sympathy for those girls because I was neglected myself as a child," she continued in that wistful tone. "If my great-aunt hadn't taken me in when my parents abandoned me, I don't know what would have happened. Maybe I would have met the same fate as poor Maya. Maybe that's why—" She glanced down at her entwined hands.

Careful. She's weaving a story her attorneys may eventually present in court.

As if intuiting Eve's reservations, Grace drew a breath and lifted her gaze. Her eyes were wide and guileless. "I don't expect you to understand, but when I stumbled across what I thought was Maya's grave, I just wanted to protect her. She'd suffered so much. I didn't want anyone disturbing her rest, especially someone as unfit and undeserving as Reggie Lamb."

No, Eve thought. *You didn't tell anyone else about that grave because you liked keeping secrets. You liked the power they gave you.* Grace had admitted as much to the FBI agent she'd taken hostage before her arrest. Now that she'd had time to plot and plan, she'd tweaked her story to have a more sensitive slant.

Eve said, "Didn't you at least think Maya's twin sister deserved some closure? You were supposed to be her friend."

Grace seemed to visibly shrink in her chair until she seemed very small and frail. Misunderstood. "It's easy to think that way now, but until you've walked in my shoes, do you really think it's fair to judge me for something that happened when I was a lonely little girl?"

Eve felt properly chastised, but in the next instant, she realized that was exactly the reaction Grace wanted to invoke. "Maybe not, but it doesn't matter anyway, since Maya Lamb wasn't buried in that grave."

Grace studied her for a long moment as if gauging an opponent's mettle. Did she find her worthy or lacking? Eve wondered.

"Unfortunately, my time with you is limited today, Detective Jareau, so perhaps you should get to the point of your visit."

"Yes, that's a very good idea," Eve agreed. "You said you spent a lot of time exploring the cave as a child. Did you ever see anyone down there? Did you ever get the sense that someone else had visited the grave?"

"The killer, you mean?"

"Anyone," Eve stressed.

She canted her head in contemplation. Her complexion was lightly tanned, Eve noted, but her hands were pale and graceful, as if she took great care to protect them from the sun. She really was a lovely woman.

There was something about her comportment and the tone and cadence of her voice that drew one in despite knowing what she'd done. Nash was right about his ex-wife. Grace Bowden was as disarming as she was cunning. The mark of a true sociopath.

"I did see someone in the cave once," she said thoughtfully. "I remember that I'd lit a candle so that I could read my book. It was always so peaceful and cool in Maya's chamber and I liked that we had our own secret place. No one ever came looking for me so I could stay as long as I wanted. That day, I'd only been down there for a little while when I heard someone in the tunnel. I was startled by the sound because the chamber was so well hidden. You wouldn't be able to locate the entrance unless you knew where to look."

"How did you happen to find it?"

"I don't even remember." Grace smiled her dreamy smile. "I like to think it was divine intervention."

Somehow I doubt that. "What did you do when you realized someone was in the tunnel?"

"I blew out the candle and hid in one of the recesses."

"Did you get a look at this person?"

"It was very dark once the candle went out." She closed her eyes on a shiver. "But there was a glow in the tunnel that grew brighter and brighter as he neared the chamber. I think he had on a headlamp. You know, the kind miners use?" Her hand fluttered to her forehead. The gesture and her tone seemed almost trancelike. "The beam caught me in the face when he stepped into the cavern. I was terrified he'd see me."

"Can you describe him?"

"No," she said in a small, breathless voice. "But his shadow on the wall looks like a monster."

Eve was taken aback by Grace's use of the present tense. She found herself leaning forward, hanging on the woman's every word. "What else do you see?" she gently prompted.

"I can't see anything. I'm pressed too far back into the wall. I don't dare peek into the chamber because if he finds me he'll bury me under the rocks with Maya. Do you think she's a skeleton by now? Have the rats picked her bones clean?"

Eve's scalp prickled. "Are you sure the person in the cavern is a man?"

That notion seemed to give Grace pause. She opened her eyes, straightened her head and said in her normal voice, "I always thought so. But now that you mention it, all I heard was a sort of whispery singsong. Could have been male or female, I suppose."

"Were you mimicking that voice just now?"

She seemed genuinely perplexed. "What do you mean?"

Eve shrugged. "Never mind. Whom was he talking to?"

"Whoever was in the grave. I thought at the time it was Maya."

"What did this person say?"

"I didn't hear anything specific. Just a bunch of mumbles. It sounded like a chant or a prayer or something. That's really all I remember. But he knew his way around the cavern and through the tunnel so he must have been down there many times before."

"You only saw this person once?"

"That I recall."

"You never saw anyone else?" Eve asked. "What about outside the cave? Anyone wandering through the woods? Any vehicles parked along the road?"

Grace sighed. "It was all so very long ago."

"You said you closed your eyes when you saw the shadow, but maybe you noticed something a split second before and don't remember. Could I show you some photographs to see if one jars your memory?"

Grace glanced behind her toward the door. When she turned back around, she looked anxious. "Go ahead."

Eve pulled the yearbook from her bag and opened it to a marked page. She turned the book toward Grace and pointed to Gabriel Jareau's photograph. "Do you remember seeing him down in the cave?"

"I don't think so. He's very good-looking. Who is he?"

"It's better if we don't use names. It's important that I get your spontaneous response to the photographs." The image of her father was meant as a test to see if she could get an honest reaction from Grace. If Eve's suspicions were correct, Gabriel Jareau had been dead and buried years before Grace had started going down into the cave.

She tapped the page. "I think I would remember if I'd seen him before. He reminds me of Nash."

The offhand remark jolted Eve. She'd never noticed even the slightest resemblance, but Grace's observation unnerved her. Had she subconsciously made the same comparison when she first met Nash? Was that why she'd been so drawn to him? Why she couldn't get over him? Or was Grace messing with her again?

Eve flipped the page and pointed to Denton Crosby's senior photo. "How about him?"

She wrapped her arms around her middle and shivered. "I don't like that one."

Eve studied her expression. "Do you remember seeing him in the cave?"

"I think I've seen him somewhere. His eyes…" She turned away from the yearbook and said in her little girl voice, "I don't like the way he looks at me."

"In the cavern?"

Grace kept her gaze averted. "Please, please don't bury me alive."

A chill danced along Eve's spine. "Grace, where are you? What do you see?"

Her voice lowered to a forced rasp. "Keep your mouth shut, you hear me? You go blabbing to anyone about what you saw down here and I'll come through your bedroom window one night while you're fast asleep. You'll disappear just like the other kid did and no one will ever know what happened to you."

Eve sat stunned. "Grace?"

She glanced around the room in confusion. Then she met Eve's gaze and sighed. "I have to go back to my room now."

"Would it be all right if I come back another day and see you? You may remember something after our talk."

"I suppose that would be okay." Grace ducked her head as if suddenly shy. "Will you do something for me, Detective Jareau?"

Eve said noncommittally, "If I can."

She glanced up through her lashes and gave Eve a knowing smile. "Tell Nash I can't wait until we're together again. Tell him I'll be waiting…no matter how long it takes."

NASH GLANCED IN the rearview mirror, automatically noting the color of the vehicles behind him on the interstate. He was still a few miles out from Tallahassee, but his foreboding continued to deepen. He told himself his trip into the city had nothing to do with Eve's visit to the psychiatric ward. She was smart and capable and he trusted she could hold her own against his calculating ex-wife.

He'd been planning a follow-up visit with Allison Forester anyway, and after attending Ron Naples's autopsy earlier, he'd carved out a little spare time from the rest of his morning to make the trip. Any new developments in the John Doe case could have easily been discussed over the phone, but he needed to have a more personal conversation with the forensic anthropologist. A casual arrangement had suited them both since their first spontaneous coffee date. No strings attached. No questions asked. But now that he'd acted on his feelings for Eve, he felt he owed Allison a clean break. His experiences with Grace had left him with an intense aversion to lies and subterfuge.

He checked the rearview again as he exited the freeway. A dark sedan had been trailing him for miles. When the car failed to follow him down the off-ramp, he told himself he was being paranoid. *Relax. No one is following you. No one is lying in wait at every corner.*

No sniper firing from a distant window. No exploding IEDs in front of him. No body parts strewn along the roadside.

He swore under his breath. He'd gone nearly a week without a nightmare and now all of a sudden his mind had gone back to that dark place in the middle of a sunny morning. Maybe everything that had happened with Grace had triggered something in his subconscious. The memories tended to come back in times of stress. Or maybe the images in his head were a graphic reminder that Eve really didn't know what she was getting into.

He rubbed a hand across his eyes and made a right turn. The lab parking lot was half-empty. He found a space near the rear entrance and showed his credentials to the guard stationed in the lobby. Allison was in her office when he arrived. He made his way through the tables of bones to the glass enclosure at the back.

She looked up in surprise at his knock, then motioned him inside. He moved a stack of files from the only available chair in the room and sat down, his gaze taking in her workspace. The cluttered desk and overflowing filing cabinets were a stark contradiction to her unruffled demeanor.

"Did we have a meeting that I forgot? Not that I'm complaining," she added with a quick smile. "I'm always happy to see you."

He sounded abrupt and businesslike by comparison. "Anything new on our John Doe?"

"Nothing to report yet. I told you I'd call you if I found anything."

He nodded. "I know, but I had some time to kill this morning so I thought I'd drive over and talk to you in person."

She tossed her pen on the desk and assessed him for a long moment. "You okay?"

"I'm fine."

"You don't look fine. What's going on, Nash?"

He wouldn't insult her intelligence by pretending ignorance. "Am I that easy to read?"

"Far easier than you like to think." Her gaze remained steady. "Are the headaches back?"

"No worse than usual."

"Are you sleeping?"

"No more than usual."

She cocked her head. "Something's not right. Are you going to make me guess what it is?"

"No guessing. No games," he said. "I came here to tell you that I've met someone."

Other than a raised eyebrow, she seemed unfazed by his blunt confession. Nash didn't know whether to be relieved or offended by her placid reaction. "Is it serious?"

"I don't know yet."

"I see." She sat back in her chair and folded her arms. "Well, since you haven't mentioned any names, you have to let me guess. You owe me that much." The corners of her mouth twitched as she held up a hand to silence his protest. "One guess, Nash. That's all I'll need. You've fallen for the earnest Detective Jareau, haven't you?"

"How did you know?" he asked in surprise.

She seemed pleased with herself. "You forget that I'm a detective, too. I'm accustomed to searching for subtleties and anomalies that no one else would notice, so I couldn't help observing the way you looked at her the other day. And the way she looked at you."

He frowned. "I didn't notice any looks."

"Then you were either blind or still in denial at the time. I might have chalked the whole thing up to my imagination if not for Detective Jareau's reaction to you. She isn't very subtle, is she? I suspect she's been pining after you for ages. And knowing you as I do…" She got up and came around the desk to perch on the edge. "You've been ducking and running as if your life depended on it. How on earth did she manage to catch you?"

"I don't think she's been pining." Nash felt oddly protective of Eve and her feelings for him. He'd been aware of her attraction ever since she'd impulsively kissed him, but she'd backed off as soon as he'd responded. For whatever reason, they'd both been ducking and running since.

Allison gave him a sage look. "Despite what you say, things must be serious if you're actually admitting you have feelings for her."

"Nothing's happened," he said. "Not yet. Maybe not ever. But I thought I should let you know where I stand. I didn't want you thinking I'd gone behind your back with Eve."

"Stop right there, Nash. Don't you ever apologize or feel guilty for moving on with your life." Her quiet ferocity made him wonder if she spoke for herself or someone else. "You have a right to see whomever you want. You and I have never been exclusive. We both knew the score when we started seeing one another. If you've found something real with Detective Jareau then I'm happy for you both."

"Thanks."

"But…" Her expression sobered as she continued to regard him. "That doesn't mean I'll stop caring about you. We've been friends for a long time, and I feel that gives me the right to offer a piece of advice."

He waited without comment.

"Be careful, Nash. Slow things down until you get your footing. How well do you even know this woman?"

He had no doubt she meant well, but his defenses shot back up. "We've worked together for six years. I know her pretty well by now."

"Maybe you only think you do."

"What's that supposed to mean?"

She gave him a careful study. "You value honesty above all else. It's why you felt the need to come here today and clear your conscience. Are you sure Detective Jareau has been completely candid with you?"

His voice cooled. "What's your point?"

"She came by the lab this morning with an interesting request."

"Eve was here this morning?"

"She didn't tell you?"

"No, but she was coming to Tallahassee anyway. Since she was already in the city, she probably wanted to see if you had any additional information on John Doe."

"She wasn't following up on the case, Nash. She came here to drop off a DNA sample."

A DNA sample? *What the hell, Eve?*

Ever since they'd left the lab two days ago, Nash had had a bad feeling she was hiding something from him. He'd wanted to believe she was just being cautious, crossing t's and dotting i's as she chased down leads. But if she'd brought a DNA sample to the lab, then she must have a pretty good idea of John Doe's identity. Why keep something that important from him?

"Whose DNA?" he asked.

"I have no idea. It was an anonymous swab. She asked me to run a comparison with John Doe and to let her know as soon as I had the results. She also asked that I not say anything to you."

"She named me specifically?" Anger bristled, but his demeanor remained cool and steady. "Did she say why?"

"She was pretty closemouthed about the whole thing. She said she wanted to be discreet in case her hunch didn't pan out."

That seemed to be her go-to excuse when she didn't want to share information. Nash didn't like what he was hearing. He couldn't imagine Eve withholding evidence just to claim credit for closing a case, but any other explanation was even harder to stomach. "What else did she say?"

"That was about it. She was in and out in less than five minutes. She said she had somewhere else she needed to be."

"Have you run the test?"

"That'll take some time," Allison said. "DNA abstraction from skeletal remains is still a delicate process. Don't expect the results for at least a week."

"Can't you rush it? This is important, Allie. I wouldn't ask if it wasn't."

She shrugged. "No promises, but I'll see what I can do."

"Thanks. Call me as soon as you have the results. Me, and no one else."

"Understood." She followed him to the door. "I meant what I said earlier. If things are just getting started with Eve, maybe you should cool it for a while. After everything Grace put you through… I don't want to see you get hurt."

Nash was as irritated with Eve as he would be with any detective who'd compromised the integrity of an investigation, but he also felt the need to defend her. Not just from a personal perspective, but as one of his own. "Eve is a fine detective. She's always been diligent and by-the-book. Whatever lead she is pursuing, she must have a damn good reason."

Despite his lofty words, he left the lab feeling blindsided. He didn't like secrets. He'd had his fill of deception with Grace. He'd ignored his instincts when it came to Eve because he wanted to trust her. He still wanted to trust her. He still hoped she had a solid explanation for her silence, but the fact that she'd kept something as significant as a DNA sample to herself made him question her motives.

It made him wonder if she was trying to protect someone.

Chapter Ten

Eve kept a watchful eye as she exited the freeway onto the two-lane highway where she and Nash had been ambushed two nights ago. That experience alone would have made her cautious, but the interview with Grace had ratcheted up her apprehension. She'd been in the woman's company for all of thirty minutes and yet she had a feeling that Grace Bowden had somehow gleaned more information about her than the other way around.

Since her arrest, Grace hadn't shown any real remorse for the kidnapping of an innocent child. What might she do if she felt threatened by another woman?

You're not the other woman. Grace and Nash are divorced. Their marriage was over a long time ago.

A fact that seemed lost on Grace.

Whatever she knew or thought she knew about Eve, she wasn't in any position to exact revenge. No matter the outcome of her hearing, she wouldn't be free to cause harm for a very long time. Denton Crosby, on the other hand, could come and go as he pleased, and he'd taken great satisfaction in proving to Eve that he could get to her whenever he wanted. He'd entered her backyard last night with seemingly no trepidation whatso-ever. If she hadn't awakened when she did, he might have found a way into her house.

She told herself his allegations against her mother were ridiculous, the wild claims of a desperate man try-ing to deflect guilt and stall an investigation so that he could cover his tracks. But the image of the shattered wineglass in her mother's hand crept back in, making Eve wonder again why questions about her father had upset her mother so much. Had Jackie known he'd re-turned to Black Creek to see Eve? Had she really kept him from his daughter?

Fingering the Mercury dime beneath her shirt, Eve let her mind drift until the peal of her ringtone joggled her back to the present. She frowned as Nash's name flashed on the screen. He knew she'd be on her way back from Tallahassee by now. Was he that anxious to hear about her meeting with Grace?

She tapped her wireless earpiece to answer.

"Where are you?"

Nash's terse question took her by surprise. He sounded…suspicious, but of what?

She told herself a guilty conscience had conjured the wariness in his voice, but her immediate leap rein-forced the need to come clean as soon as she had the DNA results.

Shaking off her disquiet, she gave him an approxi-mate location.

"Are you coming straight back to the station?" he wanted to know.

"That's the plan. Why? Has something come up?"

"Yes, but we can talk about it when you get here."

"Something about the case?" Eve tried to keep her voice even. "Nash, what is it?"

"Nothing I want to get into over the phone," he said, still in that clipped tone. "How did the meeting with Grace go?"

Eve let out a relieved breath. No wonder he sounded stilted. He'd probably been brooding about her interview with Grace all morning. "It was…interesting."

"Did anything useful come of it?"

"I'm not sure yet. But you were right to warn me about her. Grace is a very complex woman."

"That's one way of putting it," he muttered.

"I don't know what to make of some of the things she said. It was almost as if…" Eve groped for an accurate description. "She almost seemed hypnotized, as if she were recounting her time in the cave in a trance."

"Are you sure she wasn't acting?"

"I'm not sure of anything when it comes to Grace. But I'll tell you more about our meeting when I see you. Traffic is light. I should be there in twenty."

"Anything else I should know?"

"About Grace?"

"About anything. You were chasing down mysterious leads yesterday. You never told me how they panned out."

She wanted to discount that note of suspicion in his voice as projection, but something had definitely changed since they'd last talked. "I don't have anything to report yet, but I'll keep you posted."

"You do that, Detective."

Okay, she hadn't imagined that.

Why the deliberate formality? she wondered. After their intimate conversation in the garden last evening, it seemed as though their relationship had taken a new turn. This time, Nash had made the first move. This time, he'd been the one willing to throw caution to the wind until Eve had reminded him of the need for discretion in light of the upcoming hearing. Now she didn't know what to make of his chilly reserve. What had happened in the ensuing hours to alter his attitude so drastically? Or was he merely keeping a wall between their personal and professional lives?

"Is everything okay? Between us, I mean." She asked the question he'd asked the day before. "Are we good?"

"No reason why we wouldn't be, is there?" He changed topics abruptly. "You haven't asked about the autopsy."

"How did it go?"

"Preliminary diagnosis is inconclusive even though the pathologist found froth and sediment in the lungs and airways. It looks like Ron Naples drowned, but we have no way of knowing whether it was accidental."

"His car was stolen and used in a hit-and-run," Eve said. "I have a hard time believing his death was accidental or coincidental."

"You still think Ron Naples is somehow connected to John Doe?"

She thought about Denton Crosby's warning the night before, could almost feel the hard nose of his revolver pressed against the back of her skull. "I'm certainly keeping an open mind, aren't you?"

"Yes, but a lot of things don't add up," Nash said.

"Maybe not yet. Cold cases are never easy or straight-forward, especially when so much time has passed. But somebody always knows something," Eve said. "We just have to keep digging until we catch a break."

"You seem confident of a closure," Nash observed. "But if we're unable to identify John Doe, the odds are against us. Unless you have a lead I don't know about."

A long silence spooled out between them until Eve said with a sinking sensation, "You know, don't you?"

"Know what?"

She waited another moment. "You've talked to Dr. Forester. She told you I came by the lab this morning with a DNA sample."

More silence. Then, "Why didn't you tell me?"

She winced at his disappointed tone. "I was going to as soon as the results came back. At this point, it's nothing more than a hunch."

"You seem to have a lot of hunches lately, particularly when it comes to this case."

"I do have an explanation—"

His voice turned curt again. "Save it until you get back to the station. I expect a full accounting. No excuses, no more talk about hunches. I want specifics. Are we clear on that?"

"Yes, we're clear."

"In the meantime, you should know that Mr. McNally has halted demolition at the cave to give us a chance to explore. Unless you no longer feel the need."

Eve jumped at the chance. "No, I do! I still think it's important." Vital, in fact. She needed to examine the excavation site. Needed to *feel* the place where her father had drawn his last breath. Had he somehow left a clue for her? Something esoteric that had remained trapped belowground for decades? Not a ghost, but a lingering emotion. "I'm more compelled than ever," she said. *You have no idea.* "How soon can we go down?"

"I've freed up a block of time later this afternoon. See me in my office as soon as you get back. I'm serious about this, Eve. I can't have any of my detectives going maverick. We're a team here. No exceptions. You need to fill me in on everything you know about this case. I don't want to be blindsided again."

"Yes, sir," she agreed, wondering if they would ever get back to that dreamy, hopeful place they'd experienced in her garden the night before.

NASH'S DARK MOOD lingered after his conversation with Eve, but at least she'd finally admitted to keeping things from him. What those things were, he would soon find out. And if she remained evasive... Well, he'd cross that bridge when he came to it. No quarter could be given because of his feelings for her. The opposite, in fact.

His phone rang just as he pulled into the station. He parked in the gated lot and kept the AC running while he took the call. "Bowden."

"Nash?"

He tensed at the sound of his ex-wife's voice. "Why are you calling me, Grace? You know I can't talk to you."

"Don't be mad," she cajoled. "I just needed to hear your voice."

"Is Dr. Anderson aware of this call? Or your attorneys?"

"This doesn't concern them."

"Everything you do concerns them," he said in exasperation. "You're in serious trouble. You need to start acting like you understand the consequences of your actions."

"I wasn't in my right mind. You know that, Nash. You know I would never have hurt that little girl." Her voice grew small and tremulous. "I realize this doesn't excuse what I did, but I kept thinking about the child we lost. She would have been the same age as Kylie. When she came into my doll shop looking so sweet and innocent and shy…things got all confused in my head."

Nash braced himself against her manipulation. There was a time when she'd known exactly how to push his buttons, but he'd learned the hard way that his ex-wife was nothing if not a consummate actor. "You weren't the only one who lost a baby. The miscarriage affected me, too, but what happened to us five years ago doesn't justify taking someone else's child. What you put her mother through is inexcusable."

Her voice grew petulant. "I thought you, of all people, would understand. You know what's it like when things get all jumbled inside and you can't tell up from down or right from wrong. You were still a mess when we met, or have you forgotten the nightmares and flashbacks? The times I sat up with you all night when you couldn't sleep?"

He was quiet for a moment. "I haven't forgotten anything. I understand more than you think. No matter what you say now, we both know the real reason you took that little girl. You wanted my attention and you got it."

"Can you please come see me?" she pleaded.

He stared blindly out the window. "I can't help you this time, Grace. You need to start listening to your attorneys."

"Nash, please—"

"I'm hanging up now."

"No, wait!" she cried desperately. "That woman you sent to see me... Eve Jareau?"

His fingers tightened around the phone. "I didn't send her. She came of her own accord. But what about her?"

"Are you having an affair with her?"

The question was completely out of line and he was quick to call her on it. "Neither of us is married or in a committed relationship, so no, we're not having an affair."

"Are you seeing her romantically?"

He clung to his patience. "Grace, what is the point of this call? You and I have been divorced for a long time. We were separated for even longer. My private life is none of your business."

She reverted back to her trembling voice. "I'm just so afraid, Nash. I need you to tell me everything is going to be okay."

"I can't do that. You planned every part of Kylie Buchanan's abduction right down to the smallest detail, including planting evidence to make someone else look guilty. That's called premeditation. Everything is *not* going to be okay."

Her voice dropped to a hush. "I can't go to prison, Nash."

Even after all this time, even after everything she'd done, she still thought she could claw her way through his resolve. "You should have thought of that sooner."

"Why do you have to be so mean to me?"

He mentally counted to ten. "I'm not being mean. I just don't buy your act, so I'm hanging up now."

"Wait! What if I can help you solve another case? Wouldn't that carry weight with the judge?"

Nash had every intention of severing the call but instead he found himself asking reluctantly, "Which case?" Then he immediately berated himself for falling for such an obvious ploy.

"The remains that were found down in McNally's Cave. Detective Jareau showed me some pictures in a yearbook. I recognized a face."

"If you're making this up—"

"I'm not! I swear to God I saw this person in the cave. That's important, right? That could help you solve the case."

Nash wasn't buying it. Not yet. "Did you tell Detective Jareau about this person?"

"I'd rather talk to you. Can you come see me?"

The wheedling again. The constant maneuvering and bartering to get what she wanted. Some things never changed. "No, but I can have Detective Jareau get in touch with you again."

"What if I refuse to talk to anyone but you?"

"Then there won't be any reason to put in a good word with the judge."

"Nash—"

"Goodbye, Grace."

EVE WOULD HAVE fretted all the way back to town about Nash's intentions if her phone hadn't intruded once more into her thoughts. She immediately worried that he was calling her back to fire her on the spot, but the screen informed her that the number of the caller was unavailable.

She tapped her earpiece to answer and then returned both hands to the steering wheel. "Detective Jareau."

"*Eve* Jareau?"

She frowned at the deep rasp. For a moment, she thought the caller might be trying to disguise her voice. Her mind immediately went back to Grace Bowden and the way her tone had altered between fearful and menacing when she recounted her time in the cave.

Eve said warily, "Who is this?"

"I hear you've been looking for me."

Eve drew a sharp breath. "Nadine Crosby?"

"Last time I checked."

Eve glanced in the rearview mirror. The coast was clear behind and in front of her. If someone had followed her from the freeway, they were hanging back so far she couldn't spot them. "How did you get my number?"

"You've been leaving your card all over town. Wasn't hard to track you down."

Eve figured the woman had been informed of her and Nash's queries either by her former boss or her former neighbor. Obviously, she hadn't disappeared without so much as a word as they'd both pretended, but Eve decided not to press the issue. "I'm glad you called, Ms. Crosby. It's important that we speak in person. Can we set up a time and place to meet?"

"You can call me Nadine. No need to be fancy. I knew your daddy a long time ago. He talked about you so much I kind of felt like I knew you."

At the mention of her dad, Eve swallowed back her emotions and said, "Can we meet… Nadine?"

"Why do you think I'm calling? I reckon you and me got a lot to talk about."

"Name the time and place," Eve said.

"There's a gravel turnoff just past the next mile marker on the right."

Eve flashed another glance in the rearview mirror. How did Nadine know her location?

"Are you following me?" she asked.

"I've been behind you for miles. You can't see me but I'm back here."

Eve gripped the wheel. "Should I expect another flat tire soon? Are you going to try to run me down like your brother did?"

"Denny didn't touch you, did he?"

"No, but I can't say the same for poor Ron Naples." Silence stretched. "I had nothing to do with that."

"But your brother did, didn't he?"

"It was an accident," Nadine insisted. "Denny just wanted to borrow a car. No one was supposed to get hurt."

"And yet someone is dead. What happened?" Eve

asked. "Did Mr. Naples catch your brother *borrowing* his car?"

"I wasn't there. I don't know what happened. Besides, I didn't call to talk about Denny."

"Ron Naples's death is only one of many things we need to discuss," Eve said. "You used your position with King's Maid Services to let your brother into people's homes. A man is dead as a result and that makes you an accomplice. It's in your best interests to tell me exactly what happened."

"I can't tell you what I don't know." The hoarse voice sounded strained, as if she were holding back a painful cough. "Denny said he wanted to scare you bad enough to get you to back off. He needed a car that couldn't be traced back to him. Nobody was supposed to get hurt," she repeated. "I'm willing to meet with you, but I have to protect myself. If you send cop cars my way once we hang up, I'll see them long before they see me."

"How?" She must have someone up ahead watching the road for her, Eve decided. Her brother?

"Never you mind how. If you want to meet as bad as you say you do, then watch for the mile marker. Make that turn and follow the road back into the woods for another mile or so until you come to a tree with a yellow ribbon tied around the trunk. There's a burned-out car back in the bushes. You can see it from the road if you're watching for it. Pull to the side and wait. I'll call you again."

"I'd prefer to meet someplace public."

"That's not going to happen. Like I said, I've got to protect myself. No one else is going to watch my back."

She paused on a harsh cough. "We do this my way or we don't do it at all."

Eve told herself she would be stupid to even consider Nadine Crosby's terms, but instead of turning her down cold, she said, "I only have your word that you mean me no harm. What I've learned of your past doesn't exactly instill confidence. How do I know I'm not driving into an ambush?"

"You don't. You'll just have to trust me, I guess."

"Trust you?" Eve found that suggestion laughable. "That's not so easy considering the last time I saw my dad he was getting into a car with you and your brother."

"That's why you've been looking for me, isn't it? You want to hear about that night."

Eve's knuckles whitened where she gripped the wheel. "Do you know what happened to him?"

"I know some of it. I'll tell you as much as I can so long as you don't try anything funny. Come alone. That's the most important thing to get right. I get wind of the cops or anyone else tailing us, I'll disappear so fast you'll think I'm a ghost."

"Disappearing may not be as easy as you think," Eve warned.

"I still have a few friends in these parts and plenty of back roads to get me across the state line without being seen. I'll leave town with your daddy's secrets and you won't ever see me again."

"Nadine—"

"Make up your mind, girl. Come alone or don't come."

"Wait—"

Nothing but silence.

Eve knew better than to meet with Nadine Crosby in a remote location alone. She wasn't some wet-behind-the-ears rookie out to make a name for herself. She knew proper procedure. Call for backup and approach with caution. Do whatever needed to be done by the book in order to bring Nadine and Denton Crosby in for questioning.

But their arrest would mean opening Eve's mother up to a line of unsavory accusations. Not for a moment would Eve allow herself to believe that Jackie had been responsible for her father's death. For all she knew, Gabriel Jareau could be alive and well, living in another state with his second family.

But what if he wasn't?

What if he *had* returned to Black Creek to see her? What if someone had lured him down into that cave and murdered him in cold blood?

John Doe had been stabbed so violently his ribs had almost been severed. Then he'd been bashed in the back of the head with a blunt force instrument. Eve had said it herself—the sheer brutality of the kill suggested uncontrollable rage. No matter how hurt and angered Jackie had been by her husband's betrayal, she could never have attacked him so viciously.

You don't know her. Not really. Not like I do.

Eve shot another glance in the rearview. Was that a dark sedan behind her? An old pickup truck? The nearest vehicle was still too far away to identify, but Nadine Crosby was back there somewhere watching and waiting from a distance to see if flashing blue lights appeared on the horizon or if Eve instead made that turn.

Don't do it, Evie. You're smarter than that.

Was she? The temptation to find out what Nadine knew about her father was overwhelming. Eve checked her weapon and then her phone. Still plenty of battery left. Still time to call Nash and let him know what she was up to. At the very least she should alert someone of her whereabouts. She couldn't possibly be so foolhardy as to head off into the woods to meet a woman who may or may not have been a party to two violent deaths.

The turn was coming up quickly. Already Eve could see the numbers painted down the front of the mile marker post.

Don't do it.

She had every intention of speeding on by, but at the very last moment, she whipped the wheel to the right and her rear tires spun out on the gravel shoulder. For a moment, she thought she might roll the vehicle before she managed to regain control. Hitting the brakes, she rocked to a stop and took a moment to catch her breath.

She waited to see if someone came up behind her before easing across the railroad tracks. The unpaved road narrowed almost immediately. Fencerows of honeysuckle and palmettos crowded against the shoulders while hardwoods wove a thick canopy that obliterated the sunlight.

As she bumped along the road, she kept a watchful eye for the burned-out vehicle and the tree with the yellow ribbon. She spotted the ribbon first and then the car. It had been rolled into a thicket of scrub brush so that it was almost invisible from the road unless one knew where to look. Eve stopped and stared out over the rugged terrain. She wondered if the sedan might be the same car that had almost run her down on the highway, but in the next instant, she realized the model was older, and judging by the kudzu already snaking through the broken windows, it had been abandoned years ago.

Lowering her window, Eve drew in the fresh scent of the woods as she watched the road. Five minutes went by and then ten. She got out of the vehicle so she had a better view of the area around her. The place felt lonely. Abandoned. Even the songbirds sounded forlorn.

She tried to stay focused, but her mind wandered back to the holed coin found with the bones. That couldn't be all that was left of her father. That couldn't be her only clue. Something remained down in that cave and if need be, she'd search every dank nook and crevice to find it.

I won't give up, Daddy.

Some things are best left buried, Boo.

When the faded pickup truck came into view, Eve's hand automatically went to her weapon but she didn't draw. Instead, she rested her fingers on the handle as the truck stopped a few feet away facing her.

Her phone rang and she lifted it to her ear.

"Leave your gun and phone in the car and lock the doors," Nadine instructed.

Eve kept her tone accommodating. "Why don't you get out of your vehicle and we'll talk here?"

"You have to the count of three and then I'm gone," Nadine advised.

"All right, you win." Eve unholstered her weapon and placed it on the seat along with her phone. Then, lifting her shirt above her waistline, she turned slowly so that Nadine Crosby could see she was unarmed.

The truck eased up beside her. Nadine said through the open passenger-side window, "Get in."

"Where are we going?"

"Just down the road a piece. I know a place where we can talk without worrying about somebody coming upon us."

Eve glanced around. The chances of that seemed slim. They were off the beaten track and she hadn't reported in. Anything could happen on this isolated road and no one would be the wiser. She could end up disappearing just like her father had.

As if sensing her unease, Nadine said through the window, "I'm not going to hurt you."

Eve moved up to the truck. "How do I know that? How do I know you won't take me deeper into the woods and shoot me?"

Nadine shrugged. "If I wanted to kill you, I sure as heck wouldn't go about it this way. You're young and strong. You could overpower me if you had a mind to. If I was going to do you in I'd try to catch you by surprise."

She did appear frail, Eve thought. A faded gray tank top revealed her jutting collarbone and scrawny arms, and the once-platinum hair was now more gray than blond. She was Jackie's age or thereabouts, but she looked at least ten years older.

So this was the woman Gabriel Jareau had left his

family for. Eve couldn't help comparing Nadine Crosby
to her still attractive and vibrant mother.

Why her, Daddy?

No answer came to Eve.

As if sensing her unkind assessment, Nadine said
sharply, "Get in."

Eve climbed into the cab and slammed the door. The
ragged interior smelled of motor oil and mosquito repellant. Nadine hung an elbow out the window as she
waited for Eve to settle. She wore baggy shorts with
the tank top, and Eve couldn't help noticing that her
bony legs were covered with bruises. Nadine turned
her head and coughed out the window. She really didn't
seem well at all. Eve tried to harden her resolve, but an
inexplicable emotion crept in and softened the edges.
She turned to stare at the burned-out vehicle rather than
at Nadine.

The tailpipe rumbled noisily as they bounced down
the road. The sound should have grated, but Eve welcomed the intrusion because it broke the unnerving silence of the woods. She watched the scenery and tried
to keep track of how far they'd driven. Not that it would
matter if Nadine or her brother decided to put a bullet
in her skull.

About a mile or so in, they came to an old farm-
house. The yard was so overgrown with brambles and
weeds that only the top half of the clapboard structure
was visible from the road. Vines had claimed the second story, winding in through broken windowpanes and
twisting around the brick chimney. The place must once
have been lovely with gnarled shade trees ringing the

perimeter and clumps of orange and yellow daylilies popping up through the weeds. Now the derelict home looked a bit haunted.

Nadine turned the truck so they faced back out toward the road. Eve glanced over her shoulder, raking her gaze over the house and into the woods beyond. "What is this place?"

"Only place I ever truly felt safe." Nadine's breathing sounded ragged as if she couldn't pull in enough air. She turned off the engine and rested her head against the seat as her hands dropped to the worn upholstery, fingers curled upward like an anemic plant stretching toward sunlight.

Eve asked in alarm, "Are you okay?"

"Just need to catch my breath." She slowly seemed to regain her strength. She motioned out the window back toward the house. "My folks bought this property years ago when land was still dirt cheap around here. My daddy was a master carpenter," she said with pride. "He built that house with his bare hands. Me and my brother grew up here."

"Do your parents still live in the area? Is that why you came back to Black Creek?" Eve asked.

"They died when I was a kid. Hit head-on by an eighteen-wheeler as they pulled out on the highway."

"I'm sorry," Eve murmured. She didn't like this experience, this unwelcome pity for the woman who had all but destroyed hers and her mother's lives.

"We didn't have any other family and no one else wanted to take us in so we were shuffled from one foster home to another until Denny turned eighteen and got us out."

"That's a tough life," Eve said.

Nadine shrugged. "Some have it a lot worse. At least I had my brother. And later, Gabriel." She flashed Eve an uneasy look. "The three of us were family."

Eve's sympathy vanished. "He already had a family."

"He had us first," Nadine said with a hint of defiance. "We all went through high school together."

"So did he and my mother."

She nodded. "I know. I remember her."

Was that bitterness in her voice? Hatred, even? Eve hardened her gaze. "Then you must have known when my parents got married. You knew my dad had a wife and kid, yet you left town with him anyway."

"You know what they say. You can't help who you fall in love with."

"That's just a convenient excuse," Eve snapped, even as she reflected on her own feelings for Nash. It wasn't the same. He'd been separated for a long time when she finally acted on her attraction. Then she'd pretended the kiss hadn't meant anything, just an adrenaline rush that had gotten the better of her. After that she'd kept her feelings hidden until he'd come to her.

It's not the same.

Nadine's head was still reclined against the seat, her eyes closed. "He never stopped loving you. Not for a single second. He cared about your mama, too, but Gabriel was never meant to settle down. He had too much of a wild streak. He craved danger and adventure like a junkie craves a fix. We were alike in that way."

"Did you kill him?" Eve blurted.

Nadine turned her head, looking pained. "Why would I kill him? He was my heart."

"Then why does your brother want me to drop my investigation into the remains that were found in McNally's Cave? If you cared about my dad the way you say you did, why wouldn't you want to know what happened to him?"

Nadine's head lifted and her wary gaze suddenly turned piercing as she studied Eve's face. "You really don't know?"

Eve shook her head.

"You need to stop asking questions about them bones before people start putting two and two together."

"What are you talking about?" Eve demanded in frustration. "Putting what together?"

Nadine's voice lowered as if she were afraid of being overheard out in the middle of nowhere. "Sooner or later someone will figure out that we took her."

"What?" Everything inside Eve stilled. She had the awful feeling another bomb was about to explode.

"The little girl that went missing years back." Nadine's voice was a hoarse whisper. "We took her."

Eve's mind refused to go there for a moment. Then she said on a breath, "You and your brother kidnapped Maya Lamb?"

"Me, my brother...and Gabriel."

Chapter Eleven

Eve recoiled, pressing up against the door as if putting physical distance between her and Nadine could somehow lessen the impact of the woman's stunning confession. It couldn't be true. Gabriel Jareau had been a lot of things, but he was no kidnapper. Nadine was trying to save herself. *Don't believe a word she says.*

A wave of nausea rolled through Eve, and for a moment she thought she would lose her breakfast. Leaning out the open window, she drew in deep gulps of air and tried to calm her churning stomach. All the while, her mind continued to scream, *No, no, no—it can't be true!* She would never believe it to be true. Her beloved father had kidnapped Maya Lamb? *No!*

Nadine waited patiently beside her. "You okay?" she finally asked.

Eve wiped the cold sweat from her brow with the back of her hand. "I feel sick."

"I shouldn't have blurted it out the way I did. It must have been a shock. Just sit quietly and take a few more deep breaths. It'll pass in a minute."

But it wouldn't pass. The revulsion curling in Eve's

stomach was just the beginning if there was even so much as a kernel of truth in Nadine's confession.

"I don't believe you," she said as much to herself as to her companion.

"I know," Nadine said in a pitying voice. She lifted her hand as if to pat Eve's shoulder, then seemed to think better of it. She draped her arms over the steering wheel and hunched forward. "I'm telling you the truth, though."

"Truth or not, why are you telling me any of this? What do you hope to accomplish?"

Nadine rested her head briefly on the steering wheel. "I guess I thought after all this time you deserved to know the truth about your daddy."

"What's in it for you?" Eve mustered up a cold stare. "You must be trying to get ahead of something. You think if you blame my dad for masterminding Maya Lamb's kidnapping, the law will go easy on you and your brother. That won't happen," she assured her.

"I never said Gabriel masterminded anything. None of us did. And there's nothing in it for me except maybe a little peace," Nadine said in resignation. "But I don't expect you to believe that, either."

"It doesn't add up," Eve countered. "I saw him get in the car with you the night he left town. Maya wasn't abducted until weeks later."

"That's the way we planned it. Gabriel told everyone we knew that his cousin down in New Orleans got him and Denny jobs on an offshore oil rig. They'd be out in the Gulf for weeks. We knew plenty of guys from

Black Creek that worked on those platforms. No reason for anyone to doubt him."

"It was a lie?"

"We needed people to think we'd left town for good. We needed a good alibi for the night she disappeared."

Eve's mind raced as she tried to throw up roadblocks to Nadine's story. "How come there was never a ransom demand? That *is* why you kidnapped her, isn't it? To squeeze money out of June Chapman?"

"Who?"

"Maya's grandmother. You must have thought she'd pay up because the child's mother didn't have any money."

Nadine shrugged. "I don't know anything about that. All I know is that we got half the money up front, half on delivery. Denny said it was cleaner that way."

Eve stared at her in horror. "What do you mean, on delivery?"

"Somebody approached my brother a few days before we left town. They offered us a hundred thousand dollars each to nab those girls and take them to a drop point. Fifty thousand up front, the rest when we delivered them."

Eve frowned. "Girls as in plural?"

Nadine nodded. "That was the deal. We were supposed to take the pair in order to get all the money, but it didn't work out that way."

Eve thought about all the years that Thea Lamb had looked for her twin. All the guilt she must have suffered for being the one not taken. "Who paid you?"

"I don't know. Denny would never give us a name.

I'm not sure he even knew. He said this person told him about a secret organization made up of cops, feds and even some social workers that arranged for children in jeopardy to get a second chance."

"By kidnapping them?" Eve asked in disbelief.

"The way he explained it, the organization had to disappear the kids in order to save them. When things went right, it was as if they'd vanished into thin air. They were hidden away in safe houses until they could be given new names and placed in decent homes with people who cared about them. After my time in foster care, it seemed like we'd be doing those little girls a kindness."

"What about their mother?" Eve demanded. "Did you have no regard for the agony you put her through?"

"I felt bad for Reggie. I did. But whenever she started to weigh on my mind, I'd tell myself that she brought it on herself by letting creeps like Derrick Sway come into her home. Everyone knew it was only a matter of time before some pervert took advantage of the situation." She glanced at Eve. "When I thought about things in that light, it was easy to convince myself we were doing the right thing by those little girls."

"The right thing?" Eve stared at her for a moment. "You never once considered the possibility that you could be handing them over to traffickers?"

Nadine winced. "We didn't know about that kind of thing back then. Not really. It wasn't all over the news like it is nowadays. Maybe we didn't want to know. Maybe we wanted to believe we were doing the right thing because a hundred thousand dollars apiece was enough for all of us to have a second chance."

Even if Eve could swallow a word of Nadine's story, she certainly didn't buy the justification. "How did that second chance work out for you?"

Nadine answered bluntly. "Not good. We only got half the amount for one kid and cash never goes as far as you think it will. Once Denny and me parted ways, I started cleaning houses just to get by."

"If the plan was to kidnap the twins, why did you only take Maya?" Eve asked.

"Gabriel didn't show. He'd gone off by himself earlier to try to get a glimpse of you playing in the yard or something. When we got the go signal, he was nowhere to be found. Denny couldn't take both kids by himself so he grabbed the one closest to the window and brought her back here where we were all supposed to meet up. Then we were to take them both to the drop. We waited for a bit, but when Gabriel didn't turn up with the other kid, Denny went out looking for him. He had to make sure Gabriel didn't get caught or something and that the police weren't already looking for us. He came back a couple hours later with blood all over his hands and clothes."

Dread seeped into Eve's voice. "My dad's blood?"

Nadine nodded, her eyes shadowed with old grief. "He said he found Gabriel down in the cave. Somebody had stabbed him in the heart and bashed him in the head with a rock. He was already cold, Denny said. Nothing he could do but pile stones on the body and hope no one would find him until we got away."

Eve wrapped her arms around her middle. "And you believed him?"

"He was my brother. He wouldn't lie about something like that."

Of course he would lie. People did a lot worse to save themselves. "What made him think to look in the cave?"

"It was only a couple of miles from Reggie's house. If anything went wrong, we were supposed to head there to hide out until we could figure a way to get out of town. We'd stashed a little cash and some fake IDs down there just in case."

"What did you do with Maya?"

"We took her to the drop. What else could we do?" she asked in a matter-of-fact voice. "We sure as heck couldn't take her back home. She'd already seen our faces. We had to go through with our plans despite losing Gabriel."

"What happened at the drop?"

"A car came and picked the kid up. We never saw her again."

Anger welled in Eve's chest. She gripped the edge of the seat as a terrible image formed in her head. "You sat there and watched a four-year-old child get into a car with strangers?"

"Yes," Nadine said quietly.

Eve had to take a moment. "You left town that same night? Where did you go?"

"Here and there."

"San Antonio?"

Nadine blinked. "Why does it matter where we went?"

"My father sent three postcards to me after he left town. Two from New Orleans and one from San Antonio."

"I know. I was there when he sent them," Nadine said.

"The postcard from San Antonio came after the kidnapping. Did you send it?"

"We needed people to believe he was alive and well and we were all still miles and miles from Black Creek. Last thing we wanted was for someone to start asking questions about Gabriel's whereabouts. So I copied his handwriting as best I could and hoped it would be good enough to fool his kid."

"Did it ever cross your mind that Denny could have killed my dad for his share of the money?"

"He wouldn't do that."

"Your brother seems to be capable of a lot more than you want to admit."

Nadine gave her a shrewd look. "People do sometimes fool you, don't they? Even your own kin. But if Denny had wanted to kill Gabriel for money, he would have made it quick. Whoever attacked your daddy must have had a powerful grudge to do what they did to him. They say you don't know what a person is capable of until they've been betrayed by the person they love most."

Eve understood the insinuation and turned the tables. "Are you speaking from experience? Did my dad betray you? Maybe he decided he wanted to be with his family more than he wanted to be with you."

Nadine shook her head slowly. "There was only one

person besides Denny and me that even knew Gabriel was back in town that night."

Eve hardened her demeanor against the insinuation. "There's no reason in the world for me to believe you. If you are telling the truth about the kidnapping, there's absolutely no reason why I shouldn't arrest you on the spot."

"I'm telling the truth, all right, at least as much of it as I know. But if you take me in I'll deny every word of it until my dying breath."

"Why? If you really want peace, why not take responsibility for what you did and accept the consequences?"

"I can't go back to prison. Not at my age. I don't want to end my days in a cage."

"You may not have any say in the matter," Eve told her.

"No, I thought it through before I called you. Without evidence, it's your word against mine."

"There's evidence somewhere. If I have to search every inch of that cave, I'll do it. If it takes me the next decade, I'll find it," Eve promised.

"I can't stop you from trying, but it's been nearly thirty years and we made sure we covered our tracks."

"Criminals always think they've covered their tracks, but something gets forgotten or left behind. People talk."

"Maybe *you* need to think this through," Nadine said. "You keep pushing like you are and people may start to wonder if you're trying to put the blame on me and my brother to protect someone else. And for what? Take a good look at me. Do I look like I have enough time left to serve a long prison sentence? Chances are I'd be dead before they could ever bring a case to trial."

Eve gave her a long once-over. "What's wrong with you?"

"Stage four lung cancer. Nothing they can do about it. The doctors say I waited too long to come in and get checked out."

Eve stared at her for a moment longer, taking in her gaunt features and sallow complexion. "I'm sorry."

Nadine glanced away. "Don't be. Maybe I'm getting what I deserve. Even if Maya Lamb ended up with a better life, it wasn't our place to take her."

"Do you think she could still be alive?"

"I don't know. I hope so. I pray so."

Eve did, too, but they both knew the odds were not in Maya's favor.

"Why did you come back after all this time if not to turn yourself in?" Eve asked. "Surely it wasn't just to clear your conscience with me."

"I came back because Denny was here. And because I heard another little girl had gone missing."

Eve's voice sharpened. "You thought he had something to do with Kylie Buchanan's abduction?"

"Doesn't matter what I thought. You caught her kidnapper dead to rights, didn't you?"

"Yes."

"Well, then." She shrugged as if everything had worked out for the best. As if she hadn't just confessed to the crime of the century by Black Creek standards. As if she hadn't just shattered Eve's memory of her adored father.

"So what now?" she asked.

"I can't just let you walk away from this," Eve said.

Nadine's smile seemed more like a grimace. "That's what I figured you'd say. Which is why I took precautions before I came here."

"Meaning?"

"I called my brother and told him what I intended to do. He's on his way out here to try to stop me. He's probably getting close by now."

Eve glanced over her shoulder.

"You're right to be afraid of him," Nadine said with a nod. "Denny gets mean when he's cornered. But if we hurry, I can drop you back at your car and you can hightail it to safety before he gets here. Or you can wait and try to take us both in at the same time."

"So YOU LET her go?" Nash stared at Eve in disbelief.

She stared right back at him across his desk. "What would you have me do? I could hardly take on Nadine and her brother without a weapon."

"That's my point. What were you thinking, meeting this woman unarmed out in the middle of nowhere? To make matters worse, you left your phone behind so you couldn't call in for backup. Did I hear that right?"

She had the grace to look embarrassed. "I know it sounds bad."

"Damn right it sounds bad. You're a seasoned officer of the law, Eve. You had to know better."

"I knew it was a risk, but she offered information I couldn't get anywhere else. I weighed my options and decided to hear what she had to say. What would you have done in my place?" she asked in a reasonable tone.

"I would have called in my whereabouts and made sure backup was on the way." A pat answer, but he couldn't say with absolute certainty that he would have reacted any differently.

"I made a split-second decision to follow my instincts, and in light of what I learned from Nadine, I think the risk was well worth it."

Nash refused to give her a break. "And if she'd pulled a gun on you?"

"I would have handled the situation. Give me a little credit."

"I'd like to, but you're not making it easy." He leaned back in his chair, still scrutinizing her disapprovingly. "This isn't like you—withholding information on a case, refusing to call in for backup. What's going on with you?"

"Does any of that really matter given what we now know about Maya Lamb's kidnapping?" Her voice remained calm but her knuckles whitened where she gripped the arms of the chair. Nash wanted to argue that of course it mattered. Safety and conduct always mattered. Going off half-cocked was never a good look for a detective. But he conceded her point for the moment.

"Why did she come to you with this information?"

"She said she heard I'd been looking for her."

Nash frowned. "We've both been looking for her. Why call you and not me?"

"Maybe because you're the chief of police. Your position would likely intimidate someone like Nadine."

She tucked back her hair in frustration. "Again, I feel like you're missing the point."

"No, I'm just trying to get a clear picture of how this meeting went down." Because Nash still had the feeling Eve was holding out on him. "I'm trying to understand why Nadine Crosby remains a free woman."

"Even if I'd managed to bring her in, she said she would deny everything," Eve explained. "It would end up being my word against hers. You and I both know her confession would never hold up in court."

"Which is why you should have followed protocol," he couldn't help stressing.

She closed her eyes briefly. "I know. I'm sorry. But if I hadn't met with her, we wouldn't have as much information as we do." She loosened her grip on the armrests and got up to pace. "This is the first break in Maya Lamb's case in nearly three decades. At least now we know where to look for evidence and witnesses so that we can start piecing it all together. If there's even the slightest chance she's alive, her family deserves to know the truth. If she's not, they still deserve justice."

"They deserve not to have their hearts broken all over again," Nash cautioned. Eve had gone over to the window to stare out. He swiveled his chair to track her. "How do we know Nadine Crosby is telling the truth?"

"Why would she lie about something like that? She's a dying woman."

"According to her."

"I believe her. She looks deathly ill." Eve turned and leaned back against her hands. "I think she wanted to clear her conscience before she dies."

"Why did she feel the need to clear her conscience with you? That's the part I don't get. Tell me what I'm missing." Nash cocked his head as he continued to regard her. "What are you still not telling me?"

"I came straight here after my meeting with Nadine so that I could relate our conversation while it was still fresh in my head. Doesn't that count for anything?" Her gaze remained steadfast and steely, but he could detect a slight tremor at the corners of her mouth.

"What's going on with you, Eve?" When she didn't answer, he repeated the question in a softer voice. "What is it?"

She closed her eyes on a breath. "You're right. There is something else."

He waited patiently.

"Nadine told me a third person was involved in the kidnapping."

Nash stared at her in surprise. "Why didn't you mention this before? Did she give you a name?"

The silence dragged out between them.

"Eve?"

"Gabriel Jareau."

"Jareau. Is he—"

She nodded. "My father was the third kidnapper."

Nash rocked forward in his chair, stunned by the revelation. "Your father conspired with Nadine and Denton Crosby to kidnap Maya Lamb?"

Her gaze burned into his. "They were paid to abduct both girls that night. Only according to Nadine, my dad never showed up at Reggie's house."

"Paid by who?"

"Nadine doesn't know or wouldn't say. I believe my dad was double-crossed by one or both of his accomplices for his share of the money. Then he was buried beneath a pile of rocks in McNally's Cave in the hope that his body would never be found."

Chapter Twelve

Eve was quiet all the way out to the cave. For all that she had revealed to Nash, she was still holding back something important, something possibly devastating—the insinuation that her mother may have killed her father. She could barely stand to roll the possibility around in her own mind, let alone put it out in the universe for endless speculation. Before anyone else went to that dark place, she had to talk to Jackie. She had to find out if her father had really come to see her on the night of the kidnapping.

She could sense Nash's gaze on her from time to time. She hid behind her sunglasses and stared straight ahead.

He was the first to break the strained silence. "The DNA sample you dropped off at the lab was yours?"

"Yes."

"How long have you known about John Doe?"

"I still don't know for certain, but I've suspected his identity ever since that first day at the lab when Dr. Forester showed us the holed coin recovered from the grave." She pulled the Mercury dime from her collar and held it up for Nash to see. The silver seemed to shimmer with an uncanny glow, but Eve knew it was only sunlight and not magic. "My dad gave me this coin on the night he left town. He always wore one just like it. He said they would bring us luck, but I guess his ran out down in the cave."

"Why didn't you say anything?" Nash asked. "Why keep it to yourself when you knew it could change the course of our investigation?"

"I never intended to keep it from you for this long. I wanted to talk to my mom first, but then she was injured and I had to put it off. I kept telling myself I just needed a little more time, but the truth is, I didn't want to believe it was my dad down in that cave. Somehow speaking my fear aloud made it seem too real. Too final. I wasn't ready to say goodbye and, yes, I do realize how irrational that sounds."

"I get it," Nash said quietly.

The note of tenderness in his voice brought a wave of unexpected emotion. It made Eve think they might yet find their way back to the intimate place they'd tentatively explored in her garden last evening. "No matter how many years went by, I still believed he was out there somewhere, still alive and still thinking about me. It was a comfort, you know? Then to find out he'd been murdered…that someone had attacked him so viciously and buried his body down in that cave…" She trailed off. "It's hard enough to let go of a fantasy, much less to accept such a brutal truth."

He nodded, letting her ramble on for as long as she needed to.

She closed her eyes briefly. "Leaving us was one thing, but abducting a child? How am I supposed to wrap my head around that? How does one ever make peace with something like that?"

"What he did is no reflection on you," Nash said. "That's what you told me, remember? Besides, if Nadine's story is true, then your dad didn't kidnap anyone. It's even possible he changed his mind and tried to stop the abduction. Maybe that's what got him killed."

Eve wanted nothing so much as to cling to that small sliver of hope, but she couldn't dismiss or diminish the degree of her father's participation. "I appreciate what you're trying to do, but there's no way to whitewash his involvement. Even if he changed his mind, he was ready to take those girls from their home right up until the last minute. What does that say about his character?"

"*If* Nadine's story is true," Nash stressed. "We shouldn't accept her account at face value. Let's not forget that Ron Naples is dead and Nadine all but admitted that her brother killed him. At this point, they'll say anything to try to save their own hides. We need to bring them in and interrogate them separately. Make each of them worry that the other could turn."

"I agree, but they could be halfway to Georgia by now."

"We've got eyes in every corner of the county. We'll find them," Nash said with a confidence Eve was far from sharing.

She'd allowed Nadine Crosby to go free and now the weight of that decision bore down on her. What if the woman had been bluffing about her brother? If Eve had called her on it, Nadine could be sweating it out in an interrogation room at that very moment. But without her weapon, Eve had decided to play it safe and now Nadine could already be headed for the state line. Maybe she and Nash were wasting their time trawling for evidence in the cave when their efforts might be better targeted to the back roads.

"How much farther?" she asked.

"Five minutes."

He turned onto the gravel road that led back to the gated entrance. Deep tread marks from heavy equipment crisscrossed the soft earth on the other side of the fence, a grim reminder that the cave entrances were to be closed for the deadliest of reasons. Two teenagers had drowned and a man had been murdered down there. Never again, Mr. McNally had vowed. The fence and locked gate hadn't been enough to keep thrill seekers and criminals out of the cave even after the first bodies had been recovered. Blowing up the rock with dynamite and shoving the piles of debris down into the holes with a bulldozer would seal the cave once and for all.

Two uniformed officers milled about the rocky mouth that dropped nearly straight down into the first cavern. Nash pulled up behind the squad car and they got out. Eve helped him retrieve their equipment from the back of the SUV and then they went through the gate, scrambling up a gentle incline to stand at the precipice, gazing down into the pitch-black abyss.

"You sure you want to do this?" Nash asked. "Some of the passageways can get pretty dicey, and the tunnel back to the cavern is a belly-crawl for most of the way."

Eve nodded. "I can handle it."

"Just stay calm and keep breathing," Nash advised. "And don't get separated."

"I'm not about to go off on my own if that's what you're worried about."

"All right, let's do this," he said.

They used a belay rope to lower themselves down to the cave floor, pausing at the bottom to unharness and fan their flashlight beams over the limestone walls. Then they turned off their flashlights and headlamps and allowed their eyes to adjust to the sensation of total darkness.

Being belowground was an unsettling experience for Eve. Far more unnerving than she could have imagined. Close places normally didn't bother her and she hadn't been afraid of the dark since she was a child. But this was different. The blackness seemed unnatural somehow, the cool air against her face like the caress of a ghostly hand.

Daddy? Are you still down here?

No answer.

She drew a calming breath, grateful for Nash's know-how and steady presence. Otherwise, she might have crawled right back up out of that cave. The unseen walls seemed to close in on her as the distant drip of water echoed through the series of tunnels and chambers.

After about five minutes, Nash turned on his headlamp and tucked his flashlight under his belt. Eve did the same, following him silently through the first narrow tunnel into a room larger than the first. She glanced around the limestone walls and tried to appreciate the surreal beauty of the underground terrain. *This isn't so bad.* The tunnel had been tight, but at no point had she felt trapped or panicky, and the room they stood in now was spacious and ethereal.

The entrance to the second tunnel was a bit closer, the third one even narrower. Nash again took the lead, and when he dropped to his hands and knees a few yards in, Eve felt her first prickle of fear.

She was certain she hadn't made a sound, but he must have sensed her unease. He turned, keeping his headlamp averted so as not to catch her in the face. "You okay?"

She nodded then said on a thin breath, "I'm fine."

"Sure you want to keep going?"

"Yes. Don't worry about me. I'm not claustrophobic," she assured him.

"We may run into water at some point. If the tunnel is flooded, we'll turn back."

Eve was a good swimmer and had never been afraid of water, but there was no room to maneuver in the tunnel. No place to surface if a passageway flooded. And if their lights went out, they'd be operating in complete darkness. But that was the worst-case scenario, and nothing like that would happen. *Everything will be fine.*

The limestone floor grew damp as the tunnel tightened. Eve took deep breaths and tried to stay focused, keeping Nash in the beam of her headlamp. When he momentarily disappeared from her line of sight, her heart dropped before she realized he'd stepped from the tunnel into another room, this one the largest of four. The sound of water grew louder and as she emerged from the passageway, she could see the beam of his flashlight glistening on a dark surface.

"So this is the underground pool I've heard so much about," Eve said in awe. She balanced on the slippery ledge to get a better view. "This is where the FBI found Kylie's doll, trapped in a powerful whirlpool. An agent almost lost his life when Grace hit him from behind and knocked him into the water."

Eve wasn't sure why she felt the need to recount the details of Grace's crimes. Nash was undoubtedly more familiar with them than she. Maybe the kidnapping was still fresh on her mind since her meeting with Grace or maybe being down in the cave brought back the panic of those first few hours after Kylie had gone missing when the outcome of their search was still in doubt.

"The vortex could have pulled him to the bottom and no one would have ever known what happened to him," she muttered.

"I'm well aware of Special Agent Stillwell's close call," Nash said.

Eve turned. "Sorry. I wasn't trying to make a point. I guess I'm a little nervous about being down here after everything that's happened."

"No need to apologize. This place does have an effect." Nash moved up beside her and hunkered on the ledge, sweeping his flashlight beam over the water. "Grace would have known that once the doll was found we'd waste precious hours scouring every square inch of the cave."

"But how did she know the doll would be found? That's what I don't understand." Eve trained her beam straight down into the water and shivered. The pool looked bottomless. "The doll wasn't found during the initial canvas. She must have come back later and planted it, but how could she have known Agent Stillwell would come down here and take another look?"

"It was a reasonable assumption that a more thorough search would be conducted at some point. Even if the doll had never been found, she planted other clues in less obscure locations to throw us off track. She thought through every scenario."

"Sometimes it almost seems as if her instincts are supernatural." The way their voices echoed across the water drew another shiver down Eve's spine. For a moment, she could almost imagine Grace peering up at her from down below.

Nash would have none of that illusion. "There's nothing supernatural about Grace. She thinks ahead and she knows how to read people. Like any good con artist," he added under his breath.

Their headlamps were off, but Eve could see his profile in the reflected glow of their flashlights. He looked dark and mysterious. A man haunted by his past—but weren't they all?

"I can't help wondering—" She stopped abruptly.

"What?" he pressed.

"Nothing. It's none of my business."

"You want to know how Grace and I got together."

"You don't owe me an explanation," Eve said. "Besides, this is hardly the time or place."

"Maybe it's the perfect place." Nash played the light around the walls. "I can see why she would be drawn to the cave as a kid. She would have liked the darkness and the echoes." He moved the beam slowly over the water. "All those secret places."

"You would never know to look at her. The way she dresses and wears her hair…her demeanor. She seems almost shy at times."

"When it suits her," Nash said. "Nothing Grace does is by accident."

"But surely she wasn't always that way." Eve was still trying to figure out how Nash had been taken in by someone as calculating as his ex-wife had seemed earlier.

"She may not have always been capable of kidnapping a four-year-old child, but the cunning was a constant in varying degrees. It just took me a while to figure her out. Neither of us was in a good place when we met, and I think we sensed a kinship in the other. Grace seemed lost, as if she couldn't find her place in the world, and I knew that feeling only too well." He shifted, balancing the flashlight on his knee. "That's something they don't tell you when you come back stateside after combat deployment. You don't feel like you belong here anymore. There are days when you actually miss being over there. It's worse when you've left friends behind. Survivor's guilt is a very real thing."

His hushed voice echoed through the chamber, like a soft breeze whispering across Eve's nerve endings. He'd never talked to her this way before. She doubted he'd talked to anyone like this, even Grace.

"We had that in common," Nash said. "That feeling of displacement. She was different from anyone I'd ever known, and I liked that about her at the time. She didn't ask a lot of questions and she didn't mind long silences. So many people feel the need to fill every hour of every day with some kind of noise, but Grace was content to sit quietly in the dark. No music, no TV, no phone calls. It was soothing at first, that silence. Healing. I think it might have saved me. But the harder I worked to find normal, the harder she fought to keep us trapped in a void." He paused, rolling the flashlight across his thigh. "I'm not explaining it very well. Maybe after all these years I still don't understand it myself."

"There are a lot of things I still don't understand about my past," Eve said. "I've never known why my parents split up. Why my father left the way he did, why my mother gets so flustered and uncomfortable when she hears his name. Nadine's story explains some things, but it also raises more questions."

"That's why we're down here," Nash reminded her as he rose. "We should probably get moving."

Eve nodded. "I'm glad you told me about Grace. In the six years we've worked together, I still sometimes feel I don't really know you at all despite…certain moments."

He turned at that, his eyes glinting down at her in the muted light. "You took me by surprise that day."

"I surprised myself," she admitted. "Or maybe *embarrassed* is a better word."

"Why were you embarrassed? It's what we both wanted."

He said it so pragmatically and yet Eve felt her every

nerve ending react to his comment. "It was inappropriate. You were my superior and not yet divorced."

"Grace and I had been separated for years. We should have divorced a long time ago."

"I'm old-fashioned, I guess. I didn't want to do anything that would interfere with a reconciliation."

"There was never any chance of that," he assured her.

"I didn't know that, though. I backed off because it was the right thing to do and you never came near me again even after your divorce so I assumed…" She shrugged. "It really doesn't matter."

"It does to me," he said. "When this is over, I'd like the chance to show how much it matters."

Eve's heart thudded. *When this is over…*

"Let's just press on for now," she said, refusing to think farther ahead than the next tunnel. Refusing to commit when she still had her father's murder to solve. "The sooner we explore the cavern the sooner we can get out of here."

He said nothing to that, but turned to chase away shadows with his flashlight.

The interlude already seemed distant as Eve followed him off the ledge. Maybe it was her imagination, but the darkness seemed deeper now, the dank chill more pervasive as she tuned her senses to the subtle sounds of the cave. *Daddy, are you down here?*

Nothing came to her still but the faint, eerie whistle of air through one of the passageways.

GRACE HAD BEEN right about the entrance to the tunnel. The mouth was so well camouflaged that one would be hard-pressed to find the opening without prior knowledge or a guide. Eve scrambled over a pile of stones and then followed Nash into a recessed area of the limestone wall. Inside the hollow, he pointed to the black hole that would eventually lead them to the hidden chamber where the bones had been recovered.

He shined his light back into the opening. Nothing but limestone and darkness as far as Eve could see. He tucked the flashlight into his belt and turned on his headlamp before stooping to enter the tunnel. A few yards in, the walls narrowed and the ceiling dropped so that they had to maneuver the confined space bent double. Then on their hands and knees. Then flat on the floor, propelling themselves forward with knees and elbows. Another right turn and the channel tightened yet again. Eve took deep breaths, trying to control her racing pulse. She couldn't help thinking about her father's last journey through that same passageway. Had he still been alive or had someone dragged his body back to the hidden chamber for burial?

Nash said over his shoulder, "You doing okay?"

She voiced the fear that had been preying on her poise. "Are you sure we'll be able to get back out?"

"The worst is almost behind us. The tunnel should start to widen just ahead."

Eve lay flat on her stomach, arms stretched in front of her. "How do you suppose anyone found this passageway?"

"People are naturally curious about places like this. Nothing can stay hidden forever."

I'm counting on that, Eve thought.

"The walls in the chamber are covered with old graffiti," Nash said. "From what I understand, teenagers used to come back here to party until those two kids got caught in a flooded passageway and drowned. That's when the owner fenced the property and put a locked gate at the entrance. But people still climbed the fence and came down here, which is why he's now undertaking more drastic measures. But I'm not telling you anything you don't already know. You were born and raised here."

"That was before my time," Eve said. "My friends and I never paid much attention to this place."

"You were smart. It's easy to get turned around down here. Even without flooded passageways, caves are dangerous if you don't know what you're doing." Nash turned back to the task at hand, and as he'd predicted, the tunnel soon began to widen until they were able to crawl then stoop then stand as they approached the entrance to the chamber.

He hovered in the opening, splaying his light over the walls and into the deep recesses before he motioned to Eve. She took out her flashlight and turned off the headlamp as she stepped into the room. For a moment, she felt almost breathless as her scalp prickled a warning. *Daddy, you in here?*

The graffiti on the walls was faded and peeling from the moist environment. A dozen or more wine bottles with burned-out candles littered the floor, along with a few rusted beer cans.

"So kids really did come down here to party," she said in a hushed voice.

"Apparently so."

Nash remained stationary as Eve walked around the room, playing the flashlight beam over murals and dozens of personal messages proclaiming love and marking territory. Donna was here. Andy was here a year later. Carla loved Kenny nearly thirty years ago. Jackie loved Gabriel on New Year's Eve. And so on and so on...

Eve swept the beam over the messages, froze and slowly backtracked. *Jackie loves Gabriel.*

She thought at once of Denton Crosby's insistence that her mother was all too familiar with the cave. *Oh, she knew what she was doing, all right.*

Doesn't mean a thing, Eve told herself. So her mother and father had once partied in McNally's Cave. According to the messages, dozens of their contemporaries had come down here at one time or another. It meant nothing.

But what if it did? What if she not only learned that her father had been a conspirator in Maya Lamb's kidnapping, but that her mother had been responsible for his death? How would she handle such a terrible revelation? How did one overcome something that insidious? Eve didn't want to go there, but the insinuation had burrowed deep, which she assumed was exactly what Denton and Nadine Crosby had intended.

She glanced back at Nash, tracking the beam of his light as he crossed the chamber and knelt. He scooped up a handful of pebbles from the floor and sifted them through his fingers.

"This looks fresh," he said. "I think they must have already begun filling in the second entrance when I called. It was never large enough to accommodate even an average-sized adult, but I guess Mr. McNally doesn't want to take any chances." He rose and picked his way through an obstacle course of scattered stones and small boulders.

Eve watched for another moment and then turned back to the graffiti, tracing her finger slowly over the names. The message had been written on New Year's Eve in the same year her dad had graduated from high school with Denton Crosby. A couple of years later he and Jackie were married with a baby on the way. Had he already been seeing Nadine? Had he already felt trapped by the confines of marriage and parenthood? Had he considered Eve a burden from the moment she'd been conceived?

Beneath the love message, a crescent moon dangled from the word *eve* in New Year's Eve. *Each night before you go to bed, stand at the window with that lucky dime. Look up at the moon and think about me. I'll be gazing up at the same moon and thinking about you. That way, we'll always be together no matter where we are.*

The memory was almost a physical jolt. She clung to her lucky coin as she traced the outline of the moon with her finger. *I'm here, Daddy.*

I wish you hadn't come, Boo. I wish you never had to know.

She turned, almost expecting to find her father's ghost hovering behind her. Instead, she saw nothing but the scattered remnants of his secret grave. *Daddy?*

"Eve?"

She'd been so caught up in the moment that her name

so softly spoken startled her yet again. She splayed her beam over the walls in a frantic search for the disembodied voice.

"Nash?" When he didn't answer, she called in a shaky voice, "Where are you?"

"I'm here."

She moved the beam toward the sound of his voice. "Where? I can't see you."

He stepped from a deep cavity in the wall. "I'm right here. I thought I'd found another tunnel, but it only goes back a few feet."

"Do you suppose that's where Grace hid when she heard someone in the tunnel?"

"If you believe her story."

"I'm inclined to," Eve said. "You didn't see her face this morning when she recounted the experience. I could have sworn she was a frightened little girl. And, no, I don't think she's that good of an actor."

"You don't know her," Nash said.

"You're right, I don't. But let's assume she did see someone down here. She may be the best chance we have of finding John Doe's killer."

"She'll only agree to cooperate if there's something in it for her," Nash warned.

"Maybe this time she'll do the right thing."

"Don't count on it. She called me after your meeting. She said she recognized someone from the photos you showed her."

"Yes, she had a strong reaction to Denton Crosby's image. But why call you when she'd already talked to me about it?"

"She thinks if she helps solve the case, it will sway the judge in her favor."

"Will it?"

"I don't know. After what she's done?" He had just stepped out of the recess and started toward Eve when she heard a low rumble from above. She lifted her gaze to a sliver of light in the ceiling.

"Did you hear something?"

He cocked his head, listening. "Sounds like an engine."

"That close to the opening? You said Mr. McNally shut down the operation, right?"

"Yes, everything's on hold until he hears back from me."

The sound of the engine grew steadily louder.

"Maybe they're moving some of the machinery to another job site," Nash suggested.

Before Eve could respond, a small explosion on the surface sent an avalanche of rocks and debris down through the cave opening, pelting her upturned face until she scrambled for cover. Pressing against the wall, she pulled her shirt up over her nose and mouth. The air was suddenly so thick she could scarcely draw a breath.

"Nash?" She choked on a mouthful of dust.

He responded at once. "Over here. You okay?"

"Yes. Where are you?"

"I'm still on the other side of the cavern. Stay put. I'll come to you."

But no sooner were the words out of his mouth than another explosion shook the cave ceiling, dislodging a chunk of limestone that came crashing to the floor behind her. She yelped and dived out of the way. A boulder that size could have crushed her skull.

Someone above was detonating charges all around the opening. Rather than sealing the entrance, the explosions were filling the chamber with a deadly combination of rock shards and fine dust. Was that the intent? Eve wondered. To obscure the chamber where her father had been buried?

"Nash?" When he didn't answer, she fought back a wave of panic as she coughed harshly into her shirt. She eased away from the wall and peered up at the ceiling. The hole had doubled in size. Before she could duck out of the way, another avalanche rained down upon her.

She stumbled through the dust, calling for Nash. "Can you hear me?"

"Someone's using a bulldozer," he said. "This whole place is about to be filled in."

"Where are you?"

"Don't worry about me." His voice sounded muffled. "Head for the tunnel!"

Fear shot through her. "Are you hurt?"

"No, I'm okay. I'll meet you at the tunnel."

"I don't know where it is! I can't see anything through the dust."

"Keep your face covered. I'll come find you."

She tried to follow the sound of his voice, but the chaos had completely disoriented her. She'd taken only a few steps in what she thought was the right direction when something struck her on the head hard enough to knock her off her feet. Dazed, she tried to crawl to safety, but the avalanche came harder and faster, cutting off her air and obliterating her sense of direction. She couldn't breathe. Panic set in. She was about to be buried alive in the same place where her father's bones had remained hidden for nearly three decades.

Daddy?

I'm here, Boo. Just take my hand.

Chapter Thirteen

Eve had only a hazy recollection of the actual rescue. If pressed, she could call up a vague image of being lifted from the cavern through the hole in the ceiling and then gently placed on the ground by Nash and her fellow officers. By the time the EMTs arrived, she was lucid, sitting up and insisting that she was fine, though she had to admit her head hurt and her right arm just might be broken. She cradled it against her body while arguing with Nash that he needed to be out searching for Denton Crosby instead of fussing over her.

"That's being handled," Nash assured her as one of the techs checked her vitals.

"You've got a pretty big goose egg on the back of your head," the tech observed. "Could be a concussion, and that right arm is almost certainly fractured. We'll give you a ride to the ER so you can get patched up."

"I feel fine," Eve insisted. "I don't need to go to the hospital."

"Why do cops always make the worst patients?" he wanted to know.

"You're going to the ER," Nash informed her. "Head

injuries are nothing to take lightly, and besides that, I'm not about to send you out in the field with a broken arm."

"It's probably just bruised or sprained."

"We'll soon find out."

Eve put up a good fight, but in the end, common sense and Nash's stubbornness won out. Three hours later, she was ensconced in a cubicle at the hospital having undergone a series of MRIs, X-rays and EEGs. Her mother arrived just as she was wheeled back into the room from having her arm casted. She hovered at Eve's bedside, smoothing the covers and berating her daughter for not having called her sooner.

"I'm fine, Mom," Eve said wearily. "I didn't see the need to worry you."

"Thank goodness Chief Bowden thought otherwise." Jackie plumped Eve's pillow. She was composed so long as there were tasks to be done, but when she stopped long enough to observe the superficial injuries on Eve's face and arms, her eyes filled with tears. "Oh, Evie! Just look at your poor face. You were only just starting to heal from your last injury. And that arm!"

Eve held up her cast. "We're a matching pair now."

Jackie scowled down at her. "This is not a laughing matter."

"Sorry. Must be the morphine," Eve murmured. "By the way, where is Chief Bowden?"

Her mother lifted a brow as if she'd picked up on something in Eve's tone. "He hurried out as I was coming in. Police business, I guess."

Eve sat up in bed. "Did he say what it was?"

"I didn't ask. I was too worried about you at the time." She put her hand on top of Eve's. "Why didn't you tell me about the remains that were found in the cave?"

Eve lay back against the pillows. "We were trying to keep it under wraps until we had a positive ID. But I should have known better. Word always gets around in this town."

"I thought something was up when you asked about Gabriel's broken bones. Is that how you knew it was him?"

"We still don't have a positive ID, but I suspected John Doe's identity because of this." Eve pulled the dime from her collar. "Daddy gave this to me on the night he left town. He always wore one just like it, remember?"

"Yes." Jackie sniffed. "For a grown man, he had a lot of silly superstitions."

What would you say if I told you Daddy helped me get out of that cave alive?

He hadn't, of course. His presence had been nothing more than Eve's imagination. Her subconscious conjuring a familiar voice to calm her fears. That was the logical explanation.

"A holed coin just like this was recovered from the cave along with the remains," she said.

Her mother couldn't take her eyes off the dime. "Gabriel's coin?"

"I think so." Eve let the dime drop to her chest, no longer bothering to hide it inside the neck of her hospital gown. "I need to ask you something, Mom."

"What is it?"

"Did Daddy come back to town? After he left us, I mean. Did he try to see me on the night Maya Lamb went missing?"

The color seemed to drain from Jackie's face as she stared down at Eve in distress. "How could you possibly know that? You were in your room when he came. I wouldn't let him come inside."

"Why?"

"*Why?* After everything he'd done I was supposed to welcome him home with open arms? He left me with a child to raise and a mortgage to pay and he thought he could drop back in to play daddy whenever the mood struck him. It wasn't going to work that way. He made his choice." The level of her bitterness shook Eve. After twenty-eight years, her mother was still that angry?

"You had every right to send him away," Eve said. "I'm not trying to second-guess your decision. I just want to know the truth."

Jackie's blue eyes glittered with unshed emotion. "Who told you he came back?"

"Nadine Crosby."

Her mother recoiled from the bed as if Eve had physically struck her. "When did you talk to that woman?"

"This morning. Mom…" Eve searched her mother's face. "Did you know what they were up to that night?"

"What are you talking about?"

"Nadine said they were paid to kidnap Maya Lamb. They were supposed to take both twins, only Daddy never showed up after he came to see me."

Her mother stared back at her in confusion, but there

was an inexplicable darkness in her eyes, a strange note of dread in her voice. "You're not making any sense."

Maybe she wasn't, Eve thought. She was starting to mumble and slur her words. The medication was kicking in big-time. She leaned back against the pillows and closed her eyes. "Daddy left town with Nadine and Denton Crosby because they needed an alibi for the night the twins were to be taken. He wanted everyone, including you and me, to think he was miles away and that he was never coming back. But he did come back. What happened when he came to the house?"

"I already told you, I wouldn't let him inside. Not when he had the smell of that woman all over him. I would have sooner seen him dead."

Eve tried to muster up the energy to open her eyes, but she seemed to sink deeper into the pillows. She was so tired. She was physically exhausted and emotionally drained, but she needed to stay alert. Her mother had just told her something important, something she needed to remember…

She had the sense that Jackie was leaning over the bed, peering down at her. "Evie?"

"Hmm…"

"Go to sleep, sweetheart. You don't have to worry about your daddy ever again."

EVE SPENT THE night and most of the next day in the hospital, but as twilight hovered on the horizon, she got up, dressed and signed herself out. The on-call doctor had advised that she take it easy for the next several days, to which Eve had readily agreed. But she would have agreed to almost anything to get back home to her own bed. She would have called Jackie to come and pick her up, but Nash arrived just as she'd finished dressing and signing all the release forms. He'd volunteered to take her home, and once there, he insisted on staying while she settled in.

On the way home, he'd filled her in on the search for Nadine and Denton Crosby. The station had been bombarded with anonymous tips and sightings, but nothing had panned out so far.

Eve didn't want to think about them at the moment. She'd taken a painkiller as soon as she got home and now she languished in a hot bath, keeping her casted arm high and dry on the edge of the tub, while Nash puttered around in her kitchen, scrambling eggs and toasting bread. They ate on her back porch where they could watch the sunset. Afterward, they migrated out to the swing, gently swaying in companionable silence as the sky turned from golden pink to lavender and then inky blue. Stars began to twinkle through the clouds as a crescent moon rose over the treetops.

Eve thought about the crescent moon drawn on the wall of the cave. *I'll be staring up at the same moon, Boo...*

She shivered as a light breeze whispered through the magnolias, stirring a lusciously scented melancholy.

Nash draped his arm over the back of the swing, his fingertips lightly brushing her shoulder. Eve gave him a sidelong glance as she slid toward him. His arm came around her at once and he pulled her closer until their thighs touched and she could rest her head on his shoulder.

"Do you think we'll ever find them?" she asked.

"The Crosbys? We'll find them."

"How can you be so confident? Too much time has passed. They've left the state by now. They may even have left the country."

"I don't think so," Nash said. "I think they came back to Black Creek for a reason. They won't leave until they've tied up all the loose ends."

"Like me?"

"You can place the three of them together. That's not much, but it's something."

"Nadine claims my dad came to see me on the night of the kidnapping. She said Denton went out looking for him when he didn't show up. Do you think it's possible I saw them together that night and just forgot?"

He absently massaged her shoulder. "Have you asked your mom about that night?"

"She said he came by the house but she wouldn't let him in. Not after the way he left us."

"Can't blame her for that."

"No," Eve said, but she couldn't shake the disconcerting notion that there was more to the story than her mother had let on. She sighed heavily, her gaze fixated on the rising moon.

"Tired?" Nash asked.

"A little."

"Maybe it's bedtime."

The low rumble of his baritone stilled her heart. She

lifted her head so that she could see his profile in the dark. "It is getting late," she whispered.

His hand came up to tangle in her hair as he brought his mouth down to hers. The kiss was neither languid nor fiery, but a slow burn that built and built until Eve broke away on a gasp. Then she cupped his face in both hands, searching his eyes before she stood and took his hand.

He followed her into the house, pausing in the kitchen to kiss her and then again in her bedroom doorway. By this time, Eve was floating as much from anticipation as the painkiller. She got into bed and waited. Nash sat on the edge and removed his boots, then lay back beside her on top of the covers. Eve snuggled up against him and his arm came around her again.

When she would have taken their caresses to a more intimate level, Nash held back. "We need to take things slow. I've got a lot of baggage going back a lot of years. You need to know what you're getting into."

"It's been six years," she said. "If that's not taking things slow, I don't know what is."

His eyes gleamed in the moonlight. "Exactly. It's been six years. What's another night until you have a chance to think a little more clearly? Morphine and adrenaline is a powerful combination."

"I left the morphine back at the hospital and the adrenaline wore off sometime last night. My head is clear and I'm not about to change my mind."

"I'm counting on that."

She lay back against his shoulder. "You're not the only one with baggage, you know."

"Then we both need the chance to think things through."

She slid her hand into his. "I'm glad you're here." He squeezed her fingers as she nestled against him. "I feel like I could stay like this forever."

He kissed her forehead. "Sleep. I'll be right here when you wake up."

BUT HE WASN'T there when she woke up. Eve picked up her phone from the nightstand and glanced at the time. It was after seven. She couldn't remember the last time she'd slept that late on a workday.

The scent of fresh coffee drew her out of bed and down the hallway, where Nash stood shirtless in her kitchen. For a moment, she indulged herself in a delicious fantasy before he turned and said briskly, "Coffee's ready." He poured her a mug and brought it to her.

"You're not going to have a cup?"

"I need to get to the station. You okay here alone or should I call your mom to come over?"

"She has work today. Besides, I don't need a babysitter," Eve told him. "What I need is to get back to work."

He nodded to her cast. "Not with that arm. Take some time to recuperate."

"How much time?" She followed him back into the bedroom while he dressed.

"As much time as the doctor says you need." He kissed her forehead as he buttoned up his shirt. "I'll call you later."

"Nash, wait." She trailed him back out of the bedroom and down the hallway to the front door. "Why are you in such a hurry? What's going on?"

"I'm running late. I'm always in the station by seven."

"If you don't tell me what's going on, I'll get dressed and come down to the station myself."

"You would, wouldn't you?" He tucked back a strand of her hair. "Nadine Crosby just turned herself in."

"What? When?"

"A few minutes ago. She says she'll only talk to the person in charge. Says she wants to cut a deal."

"She's turning on her brother?"

"Unless this is some kind of ploy the two of them have cooked up. We'll soon find out."

"You have to let me come with you," Eve said. "I'm the one she talked to before. Maybe she'll want to see me again."

"If I need you, I'll call you. Right now the best thing you can do is rest. I don't need to remind you that you'll have to qualify with that arm, so take care of it."

She relented but only because she wasn't yet dressed. She hurried back to the bedroom to throw on jeans, sneakers and a T-shirt before heading out. She was on the front porch struggling to lock the door with her left hand when a FaceTime call came in. Grace Bowden's image appeared on her screen.

Eve couldn't have been more shocked. "Grace? How did you get my number?"

"You left your card, remember?"

"Did I?" Eve didn't think she had, but she didn't press the issue. "Why are you calling?"

"I want to see those photographs again. The year-book photographs? I've remembered something."

Eve glanced over her shoulder to scour the street. She didn't think that Denton Crosby would be so bold as to show up at her house in broad daylight, but after he'd tried to bury her alive in the cavern, he might be desperate enough to try anything.

"What's going on?" Grace wanted to know. "You seem flustered."

"I was just on my way out. Hold on a minute." Eve opened the door and walked back inside. Retrieving the yearbook from a bookshelf, she carried it over to the table and sat down to open the cover.

She positioned the phone so that Grace could see the page, then tapped the photograph of Denton Crosby. "You seemed to recognize this man yesterday You saw him down in the cave at some point, didn't you? He threatened you, told you if you said anything about what you'd witnessed, he'd come through your bed-room window and abduct you the way that Maya Lamb had been taken."

Grace nodded. "When I saw you yesterday, the memory was only a glimmer, but I remember more clearly now. He caught me spying on him in the cave. He grabbed my hair and hauled me out of the alcove. I thought he was going to kill me."

"How old were you then?"

"I don't remember exactly. Ten or thereabouts."

"Had you seen him down in the cave before?"

"Yes, several times, but he never saw me until that day."

"Are you sure it was this man?" She pointed again to Denton Crosby's image.

Grace squinted as if trying to get a better look through the camera. "No, not him. The photograph above him. *That* man. He's the one who attacked and threatened me."

Eve turned the yearbook around and ran her finger down the page, pausing on Denton Crosby's image. Then she lifted her gaze to the photograph above him. Her heart started to flail as she picked up the phone. "Grace, are you sure it was him?"

"Of course I'm sure. Is this going to help solve your John Doe case?".

Eve's heart was beating so hard by this time she could barely think. She felt a cold sweat break out at her temples. "I'm going to have to call you back, Grace."

"No, wait!"

"What is it? Did you remember something else?"

Grace paused. "No, it's just…" She seemed to peer over Eve's shoulder. "Who's that behind you?"

"What?" Eve glanced over her shoulder, scanning the room behind her and peering into the shadowy hallway.

"I saw someone behind you," Grace insisted. "Someone's in your house, Detective Jareau. I think he's the man in the photograph."

Chapter Fourteen

Eve tried to keep her tone neutral even as her pulse raced. "I have to go now, Grace." She severed the call and punched in Nash's number.

Before the call connected, a familiar voice said from the hallway, "Put the phone down, Evie."

She turned slowly, blood pounding at her temples. "I told you never to call me that."

Wayne Brody leaned a shoulder against the door frame and regarded her with a mixture of amusement and anger. "You have no idea how much you reminded me of Gabriel just now. He used to give me that same look of contempt. Even in high school, he always thought he was better than me, cooler than me, when he was never anything but a petty criminal."

"You showed him, didn't you?" Eve's gun was on the console table in the foyer. If she could maneuver around… "You killed him the night he came back to town. You saw him at the house, followed him down to the cave and murdered him in cold blood. Why?" The answer came to her in a flash. "You were in love with my mother."

"It was always Jackie," he said. "I've loved her for as long as I can remember. The three of us could have been a family. I would have taken care of you the way Gabriel never could. But you wouldn't give me a chance, would you? You thought you were better than me, cooler than me. No matter how hard I tried, you looked at me the way he always looked at me."

Eve took a tentative step toward the foyer. "I was just a little kid. You can't blame me for the failure of your marriage. My mother should never have married you. She never got over my dad."

"That's a lie!"

She lunged for the gun as he lunged for her, ruthlessly grabbing her casted arm. The plaster did little to protect the fracture as he wrenched her arm behind her. She fell backward in agony, banging her head on the sharp corner of the console table. Blood ran down into her eyes as she cradled her arm and suppressed a scream.

He grabbed her injured arm and yanked her to her feet. Eve's training kicked in then and she fought him, using momentum and surprise to slam him to the floor. She grabbed a porcelain vase and smashed it against his head. When she dived for the gun, he grabbed her by the ankle and pulled her back down to the floor. She was dizzy now from pain and blood loss. He took advantage of her weakness, grabbing her hair and hauling her into the bathroom. The window was open. He must have crawled through while she'd been outside.

"What are—"

"What I should have done years ago when you were

a bratty kid." He gritted his teeth as he forced her to her knees beside the bathtub. "They'll think you took too many painkillers and fell asleep in the bath. You already look like hell, so a few more cuts and bruises won't be noticed." He put in the stopper and turned on the water full blast, pushing her head down into the tub as the water began to rise. "You may have gotten out of that cave in one piece, but today is the day your luck runs out, Evie. Just like it eventually ran out for Gabriel."

Eve struggled to get away, but he had the upper hand. He held her head under until her lungs screamed for air and her strength continued to wane.

Still she fought him, thrashing her head from side to side, flailing her hands wildly until his hold slipped and she came up gasping for breath even as she swung her casted arm for his head. She must have connected because the plaster shattered and Wayne fell backward on the tile floor, cracking his temple against the edge of the tub.

Protecting her arm against her body, she stumbled out of the bathroom and limped down the hallway to the foyer to throw open the front door. Jackie stood with her hand lifted as if getting ready to knock. She took one look at Eve and gasped.

"Evie! What happened?"

"Mom, we have to get out of here."

When she would have collapsed, Jackie put her arm around her waist for support. "We have to get you back to the hospital—"

"You're not going anywhere, either of you."

Jackie's gaze shot to the hallway, where Wayne stood with Eve's gun.

"Wayne? What on earth—"

"Get out of the way, Jackie. This has gone on long enough. Let me end it."

"What are you talking about? Wayne, put down that gun this instant!"

"I wish I could, but it's too late for that. I don't want to hurt you, Jackie. I never wanted to hurt anyone. I just needed you to realize that I was your soul mate. I'm the one you should have married, not him."

"Wayne—" Jackie looked helplessly from her ex-husband to Eve. Understanding dawned and her voice softened. "Put down the gun, Wayne. Please. Let Evie go. You and I can talk for as long as you like."

"It's too late for talk. Just let me finish this. There's no hope for us so long as she's around. Look at her. She's the spitting image of Gabriel."

"There's no hope for us if you hurt my daughter."

"Why couldn't you just love me?" he asked in tears. "Why did you have to make me prove myself to you?"

"How did you prove yourself?" Jackie asked gently.

"You know how. You've always known."

Jackie drew a breath. "You killed Gabriel."

"It's what you wanted. I heard you say so."

"I never meant—" She stopped and drew another breath. Eve realized too late that her mother had been slowly inching her body in front of hers. If Wayne fired, she intended to take the bullet.

From her periphery, she saw a shadow move on the front porch. She and Jackie were still standing in the doorway so that Wayne's view was blocked. He couldn't see Nash easing around the corner to put himself in position. Their gazes met and Nash nodded.

"Mom," Eve said under her breath. "Drop to your knees."

"Wh—"

Eve collapsed, taking her mom down with her. Before Wayne could get off a round, Nash stepped into the doorway and fired.

Chapter Fifteen

Two weeks later, Nadine Crosby was dead and her brother, Denton, remained a free man. She'd collapsed at the police station before making an official statement and confession and had been rushed to the hospital, never to awaken from a coma. Everything she'd told Eve that day in the woods remained inadmissible. With two of the three conspirators dead, the chances of convicting Denton for Maya Lamb's kidnapping remained slim, and without any physical evidence or eyewitnesses connecting him to Ron Naples's death, murder charges would not be forthcoming. Eve was beyond frustrated but no less determined to find justice for the victims' families.

As for Wayne Brody, he'd been transferred to the county lockup as soon as his injuries healed. Jackie refused to see him. She was a changed woman since the shooting. Moody and withdrawn. Eve told herself it was understandable. Finding out her ex-husband had killed her first husband because he'd been secretly in love with her since high school was a lot to process. Sometimes in the dead of night, something Wayne had said came back to haunt Eve. *You know how. You've always known.*

She thought about his insinuation now as she stared out the window, unable to sleep. Behind her Nash stirred in bed.

"What is it?" he asked drowsily.

"I can't sleep."

"I'm the one with insomnia, remember?" He threw off the covers and came to stand behind her at the window. Wrapping his arms around her, he pulled her back against him. "What's going on?"

"I thought the truth would feel different," she said.

"You thought it would bring closure." He rested his chin on the top of her head. "Doesn't always work out that way, does it?"

"How do you cope?" she asked. "With Grace. With what happened over there. With everything."

"Most of the time, not very well," he said candidly. "Lately, when things get bad, I think about you. I remind myself how lucky I am that I made it back home and that I get to spend my days with the woman I love. My nights, too, when I'm especially lucky."

She let her head fall back against his shoulder. "We are lucky." She touched the coin beneath her nightgown as her gaze lifted to the moon glimmering above the treetops.

Goodnight, Boo. Have a happy life.
Goodbye, Daddy.

* * * * *

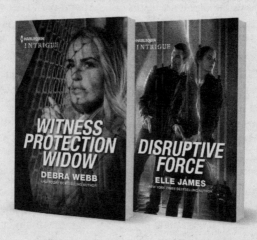

COMING NEXT MONTH FROM

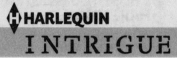

HARLEQUIN
INTRIGUE

#2055 CONARD COUNTY: MISTAKEN IDENTITY
Conard County: The Next Generation • by Rachel Lee
In town to look after her teenage niece, Jasmine Nelson is constantly mistaken for her twin sister, Lily. When threatening letters arrive on Lily's doorstep, ex-soldier and neighbor Adam Ryder immediately steps in to protect Jazz. But will their fragile trust and deepest fears give the stalker a devastating advantage—one impossible to survive?

#2056 HELD HOSTAGE AT WHISKEY GULCH
The Outriders Series • by Elle James
To discover what real life is about, former Delta Force soldier Joseph "Irish" Monahan left the army and didn't plan to need his military skills ever again. But when a masked stalker attempts to murder Tessa Bolton, Irish is assigned as her bodyguard and won't abandon his mission to catch the killer *and* keep Tessa alive.

#2057 SERIAL SLAYER COLD CASE
A Tennessee Cold Case Story • by Lena Diaz
Still haunted by the serial killer she couldn't catch, police detective Bree Clark doesn't hesitate to accept PI Ryland Beck's offer of redemption. The Smoky Mountain Slayer cold case has gone hot again and working together could bring the murderer to justice. But is the culprit the original slayer—or a dangerous copycat?

#2058 MISSING AT FULL MOON MINE
Eagle Mountain: Search for Suspects • by Cindi Myers
Deputy Wes Landry knows he shouldn't get emotionally involved with his assignments. But a missing person case draws him to Rebecca Whitlow. Desperate to find her nephew, she's worried the rock climber has gotten lost...or worse. Something dangerous is happening at Full Moon Mine—and they're about to get caught in the thick of it.

#2059 DEAD GIVEAWAY
Defenders of Battle Mountain • by Nichole Severn
Deputy Easton Ford left Battle Mountain—and the woman who broke his heart—behind for good. Now his ex-fiancée, District Attorney Genevieve Alexander, is targeted by a killer, and he's the only man she trusts to protect her. But will his past secrets get them both killed?

#2060 MUSTANG CREEK MANHUNT
by Janice Kay Johnson
When his ex, Melinda McIntosh, is targeted by a paroled criminal, Sheriff Boyd Chaney refuses to let the stubborn officer be next on the murderer's revenge list. Officers and their loved ones are being murdered and the danger is closing in. But will their resurrected partnership be enough to keep them safe?

YOU CAN FIND MORE INFORMATION ON UPCOMING HARLEQUIN TITLES, FREE EXCERPTS AND MORE AT HARLEQUIN.COM.

HICNM0122B

Chapter One

Maintaining a white-knuckle grip on the steering wheel while
negotiating the treacherous curves up Prescott Mountain on his
daily commute was typical for Ryland Beck. *Smiling* while he
resolutely refused to look toward the steep drop on the other
side of the road *wasn't* typical. Nothing, not even his phobia
of heights, could dampen his enthusiasm this chilly October
morning. Today he'd begin his investigation into a serial killer
case that had gone cold over four years ago.

Bringing down the Smoky Mountain Slayer was the challenge
of a lifetime. No suspects. No DNA. No viable behavioral
profile. In spite of the lack of evidence, Ryland was determined
to put the killer behind bars. He wanted to give the families of
the five victims the answers and justice they deserved.

Unfortunately, what he couldn't give them was closure.
Closure, as he well knew, was a fictional construct. The death of

a loved one would always leave a gaping hole in the hearts and lives of those left behind. But knowing the victim's murderer had been caught and punished would go a long way toward making the excruciating grief more bearable.

He continued winding his way up the mountain toward UB headquarters as he considered the limited information he'd found on the internet about the killings. The Slayer's modus operandi was consistent: all of his victims were strangled, their bodies dumped in the woods in Monroe County. But aside from them being young women, the victimology was all over the place. Their educational and economic backgrounds varied, as did their ethnicity. Some were married, some weren't. Some had children, some didn't. All of that made it nearly impossible to build a useful profile to help figure out who'd murdered them.

The detectives from the Monroe County Sheriff's Office had deemed the case unsolvable. But here in Gatlinburg, Ryland had a unique advantage: an über-wealthy boss who knew firsthand the suffering a victim's family endured when a murder case went cold.

Seven years after his wife was killed and his infant daughter went missing, Grayson Prescott had given up on the stagnant police investigation. He decided to create a cold case company called Unfinished Business. Just a few months later, UB had solved the case. Now, the thirty-three counties of the East Tennessee region had formed a partnership with UB and were clamoring for them to work their cold cases.

Don't miss
Serial Slayer Cold Case *by Lena Diaz,*
available March 2022 wherever
Harlequin books and ebooks are sold.

Harlequin.com

Interim police chief Marcus Price is captivated by newcomer Erin McGarry, who has come to Knoware to help her sick sister. But he has his hands full with a string of robberies and a credible terrorist threat, and he's not confident that Erin didn't bring the danger to the small community or that either one of them will survive it.

Read on for a sneak preview of
Trouble in Blue,
the next thrilling romance in Beverly Long's Heroes of the Pacific Northwest series!

Marcus watched as she got to her feet. He was grateful to see that she was steady.

"Can we have a minute?" Marcus asked Blade.

"Yeah. Hang on to her good arm," his friend replied. Then he walked away, taking Dawson with him.

"What?" she asked, offering him a sweet smile.

"I'm going to find who did this. I promise you. And you're going to be okay. Jamie Weathers is the best emergency physician this side of the Colorado River. Hell, this side of the Missouri River. He'll fix you up. But don't leave the hospital until you hear from me. You understand?"

"I got it," she said. "I'm going to be fine. It's all going to be fine. I barely had twenty bucks in my bag. He didn't even get my phone. I had that in my back pocket. Nor my keys. Those were in my hand. So he basically got nothing except the cash and my driver's license."

Things didn't matter. "You want me to let Brian and Morgan know?"

"Oh, God, no. Please don't do that." She looked panicked. "Morgan can't have stress right now. I'm grateful that her room is on the other side of the building. Otherwise, she could be watching this spectacle."

They would want to know. But it was her decision. And she was in pain. "Okay," he said, giving in easily.

"Thank you," she said.

"Go get fixed up. I'll talk to you soon."

She nodded.

"And, Erin…" he added.

"Yeah."

"I'm really glad that you're okay."

Don't miss
Trouble in Blue *by Beverly Long,*
available March 2022 wherever
Harlequin Romantic Suspense
books and ebooks are sold.

Harlequin.com